Also by Patricia Volk

Stuffed: Adventures of a Restaurant Family
All It Takes
White Light
The Yellow Banana

To My Dearest Friends

TO MY DEAREST FRIENDS

•

PATRICIA VOLK

Alfred A. Knopf　　New York 2007

This Is a Borzoi Book Published by Alfred A. Knopf

All rights reserved. Published in the United States by Alfred A.
Knopf, a division of Random House, Inc., New York, and in
Canada by Random House of Canada Limited, Toronto.

www.aaknopf.com

Knopf, Borzoi Books, and the colophon are registered trade-
marks of Random House, Inc.

Grateful acknowledgment is made to A. P. Watt Ltd. for the use
of excerpts from "An Irish Airman Forsees His Death," "Never
Give All the Heart," "The Pity of Love," and "The Song of
Wandering Aengus" by W. B. Yeats. Reprinted by permission of
A. P. Watt Ltd. on behalf of Michael B. Yeats.

Library of Congress Cataloging-in-Publication Data
Volk, Patricia.
To my dearest friends / Patricia Volk.—1st ed.
p.   cm.
ISBN: 978-0-307-26360-5 (alk. paper) 1. Middle-aged women—
New York (State)—New York—Fiction. 2. Female friendship—
Fiction. 3. Manhattan (New York, N.Y.)—Fiction. I. Title.
PS3572.O393T6 2007
813'.54—dc22   2006048718

Manufactured in the United States of America
First Edition

for

Starr Scott Brin 1943–1972
Marilyn Kosossky Greenberg 1935–1998
Karen Zissu Magidson 1947–2000

"Happiness is equilibrium. Shift your weight."

—TOM STOPPARD, "The Real Thing"

To My Dearest Friends

Overheard at the Funeral

"Who are all these people?"

"They call them *cre*mains?"

"Isn't Zabar's near here?"

"The daughter could use a little makeup."

"No wake?"
"They don't do that."
"Oh, who the hell wants to get laid out anyhow."
"The Pope."

"You knew her since Lamaze?"

"Who are all these people?"

"I went to one last week, four people showed."
"I went to one, it was me and the doorman."

"What's the husband do?"
"Surgeon."
"Can you introduce me?"

"Isn't that the lady from the secondhand store?"

"Think he'll sell the apartment?"

"Nice flowers."
"You've never seen the rose blanket."

"Who are all these people?"

"Moral of the story? Always find a therapist younger than you are."

" 'What made us dream that he could comb gray hair?' "

"I haven't seen a jacket like that since Margaret Rutherford."

"How much longer?"
"Someone's dead. Just be glad you're here."

"There's nothing like a good funeral."

"Who are all these people?"

1 · Alice Wakes

Naked Charles pads from his shower to his semainier. He would not dream of turning on our light. Charles assumes I am asleep. After so many years, he senses his way in the dark.

He slides a drawer, raising both pulls so it whispers. He extracts jockey shorts I fold so no seams show, each pair a white tuffet, his small daily gift. When we were newlyweds, Charles stood on one foot, then the other, a flamingo. Now he pulls his shorts up leaning against the wall. Someday he will collapse on our slipper chair, use his cane to spread the leg holes, then inch them up his calves. It is a privilege to watch your partner over time.

> *If soul may look and body touch,*
> *Which is the more blest?*

Yeats knew.

Charles steers his right foot in. I glimpse the silhouette of his bobbling apparatus. How perverse to cage it in clothes. All that flagrant manhood neatly squared away. He stretches on his undershirt. Watery light sculpts the muscle range of his back. No matter how soft Charles gets around the middle, his bent back stays bandy.

All these years and there's pleasure yet watching him.

In the kitchen, Charles has put up coffee. I take a cup back to bed. November sun stipples trees along the Hudson. Leaves wink like

5

sequins. Today will be perfect. There are, in a good year, perhaps ten such days in New York. They have nothing to do with temperature. They can come any season. No one can predict them. On these days the air is supercharged. There is more of something vital in it. People breathe deeper, walk taller. They pause to fill their lungs and smile without premeditation. Dogs high-step, their tails thrum. On these days the bus driver keeps the doors open when he spots you running.

Along Riverside Drive joggers wear down-filled vests, no gloves, no watch caps. Wind billows hair but not enough to backhand. I won't need a coat. The gray cashmere scarf, perhaps. In my date book I check off yesterday:

RUN
NOTES W. YUMI
SKIM, COF. FILTERS, COMET
LUBA CHECKS
CALL MR. FLEISCHMAN

A slash through each except Fleischman.

Today is wall-to-wall appointments.

10 MR. OLIPHANT: 230 CPS

I'll have to go downtown, miss my run. Why would Roberta's lawyer want to see me? Does Betsy need a guardian? Betsy is thirty-one. Jack is alive. Oh Roberta. My poor darling.

11:30 MRS. VANDERVOORT

Mrs. Vandervoort. Normally I don't open the shop till noon but Mrs. Vandervoort is terrified someone will see her in Luba and her things are awfully good. Luba is about nothing if not discreet accommodation.

FALL BAGS

How did that happen? Bags of winter inventory up to the ceiling. Here it is, almost December. They should have been on the floor after Labor Day.

CALL CAMILLE

She's due January ninth. Could the baby's head be down? What if they ask us to participate in the birth? Is that an invitation one can decline?

TURKEY SAND/MOTHER

6 p.m. CLAUDIO'S

MADAMA BUTTERFLY!

A jam-packed day. Should I cancel the lawyer? Reschedule for late afternoon? Better to get it over with. Surely Roberta didn't leave me anything else. She gave me a bracelet. Our last lunch at Café on 5.

"Alice." She undid the clasp. "I want you to smile every time you look at it. You've got to promise me. Stop shaking your head, Alice."

"I don't want it, Roberta." I said. "Keep it. Please. You're going to need it."

"Right." She grabbed my wrist with stunning strength. "And O.J. was innocent."

What would I have left you if I died first, Roberta dear? You coveted my shagreen eyeglass case. You never failed to admire Grand-mère's lava-cameo bracelet. How I wish I had given it to you.

Gray silk blouse, gray cardigan. I prefer clothes the colors of the inside of an oyster shell. Gray slacks. I will make the most of this inconvenient morning. I will walk over to Broadway, pick up bagels for Mother at H&H, drop them with her doorman, then cut through the park at Seventy-second, take the West Drive, and exit on Central Park South. I'll bring the puzzle, in case Roberta's lawyer keeps me waiting. Then catch a Limited bus up Madison and be at Luba in plenty of time for Mrs. Vandervoort.

Marvelous coffee. Italian roast from Zabar's. One peaked tablespoon per cup. Charles knows how I like it. The beauty of a mar-

riage is its ongoingness. The staying together, the sharing of history, the appreciation of wrinkles and sag in flesh once known in its
taut prime. And the longest stretches of all, the plowing comfort of
the quotidian, intimacy with all its lows and reprieves. Marriage is
like liver. It regenerates.

2 · Nanny Gets Up

It takes a crazy man to make a woman feel alive.

I roll toward you, launch an exploratory toe.

The sheets are ice.

Every morning it's news. Every morning is Day One. Not that I dream you're alive then wake up *only to discover.* Every night my cerebellum crashes. If you've been married to someone for thirty-two years and he's been dead three, how long does it take to get used to waking up alone? Is there a formula? $32+3-x<365>:58+y=z$?

Thirty-two years and you croaked on me.

Something important is happening today. What time is it? What good is a clock without glasses? Why don't glasses have locator buttons like the phone? You press a button, your glasses beep and . . . There they are—innocent by the toaster. A locator for the phone book too. The cell. One giant locator screwed to the wall so you can locate the locator. The Master Locator. That's it. I'll make a mint. Missing glasses, the basic—no, innate—no, *intrinsic* irony: how can you find them if you need them to see them?

I'm supposed to be somewhere. Something important is happening today. Maybe they're in the duvet. Shake it and stuff flies out: books, socks, spoons. Our bed, *my* bed, it's the office now. Office, dining room, library. If three rooms fell off this place I'd never know. The bed is control central. Everything that matters takes place on it. Except what used to matter.

Bobbie. The important thing has to do with Bobbie.

9

Think. Take it slow. Rule out places 100 percent the first time so you don't have to go back. Not on the end table.

End table done.

Think, Nanny. You got into bed at ten-thirty. Finished the *Times*. Turned out the light. Ah. Still on my head.

6:28.

I clomp into the kitchen and by the time I reach the coffee-maker my ankles are broken in for the day. While it drips, I wake up my computer, hit the folder marked CALENDAR, and read November 20.

10—Mr. Oliphant—230 CPS. Right.

"Dear Mrs. Wunderlich," the letter said. "I represent the estate of the late Roberta Heumann Bloom."

I don't get it. Why does Bobbie's lawyer want to see me? She already gave me the bracelet. Who knew she had a lawyer? Who knew she had an estate? Two weeks ago she was alive.

12:30—Glogowers—1136 Park

The Glogowers. Got to find them a place. Meredith's six months. Breaking my heart, these Glogowers.

3:30—the Kleckners—22 E. 87

Ken and Ricki. Royal pain.

Maybe she left me money. Wouldn't that be something. I was her best friend. Bobbie worried about me and money.

"He's tapping his TIAA-CREF?" she marveled. "Fred's taking money out of his retirement fund?"

"He earned it, Bobbie."

"That's not the point, Nanny."

What really made her nuts were our taxes.

"Let me get this straight. He points, you sign? You're telling me you don't look?"

And I'd say, "If I can't trust Freddy, who can I trust?"

"Nanny"—she'd roll her eyes—"trust is not the issue."

· · ·

I print out today's page and put it in my bag. In the bathroom, I wash my face—or, rather, cleanse it. In Makeup Court, soap gets you the chair. According to Flora, you must splash warm water, pat dry, dab on grapefruit cleanser, rinse, pat dry again, follow with kiwi toner to neutralize the pH factor, then study face in a 6X mirror. Not for the fainthearted.

"If no one can see I have one white hair on my chin, why do I have to tweeze it?" I asked my daughter. "Why do I have to see what's wrong with me six times larger? Nobody looks at me with 6X magnification."

Daily face inspection. Someone cares what I look like, even if it's only me. Not that aging is bad. So you worry about a hair on your chin instead of a pimple. So your ankles are a little stiff in the morning instead of cramps five days a month. Aging is merely a substitution of things that alarmed you then for things that alarm you now. All of life has equal alarm weight. What should I be grateful for now that I don't realize? What am I taking for granted one day I'll miss? Knees! I never think about my knees! Women my age, women younger, have to ratchet out of a cab.

Bobbie's lawyer. Jeez I hope it's money.

3 · Reckless Speculation

The carpet in the lawyer's office is the same gray as the walls. Mrs. Vogel is in pale gray as well, gray slacks, gray shirt, gray scarf. Her hair too is gray, pulled back in a peruke. With the exception of pink lipstick, her face is unadorned. It is, however, marked by a startling symmetry. This is emphasized by clifflike cheekbones, smoothly arched brows, a long Roman nose, and full lips the precise width of her nostrils. In younger people her build is called "leggy," in middle age "rangy," in older people "spindly." Once she was beautiful. Now she is handsome. Sun glints off a metal identification bracelet on her wrist. It is engraved with the words:

> ALLERGIC TO FISH
> WEARING CONTACT LENSES

On a round coffee table a vase explodes with hellebores, hydrangea and white digitalis. The arrangement owes nothing to nature. Were it summer, they could not be in bloom together. Mrs. Vogel cocks her head, studies the flowers. She leans in, checks if the receptionist is watching, then crushes a solitary petal between her thumb and forefinger, testing whether it is real. Beside the flowers, fanned vertically are copies of *U.S. News & World Report, Autoweek,* and the *Harvard Business Review.* Mrs. Vogel adjusts the creases in her slacks and crosses her legs. She removes a silver ballpoint from her handbag. Using her upper knee as a desk, she labors over the Sunday *New York Times* crossword puzzle.

.   .   .

The elevator opens. No one comes out. The doors start to close, then bounce off a woman's shoulders. "Jeez Louise!" she blurts. Disgorged, she jabs her cell phone.

Mrs. Vogel looks up. She observes the woman's shapeless black suit and recognizes the lapels. It is a DKNY from 2002. She takes in the black velvet flats with gold-embroidered tigers. They remind her of bad Greenwich Village paintings from the sixties. It is her opinion that women with well-developed calves would do well to wear pants. If they insist on skirts, then kitten heels to lengthen the leg. She observes that the woman moves well, her body is toned. She feels it is most unfortunate about the makeup. Many women make the same mistake. The older you get, in fact, the less you need.

The woman in the velvet shoes slaps her cell phone shut. She walks over to the receptionist and says, "Hi. I'm Nanny Wunderlich."

The receptionist nods toward the seating area. "He'll be with you shortly, Mrs. Wunderlich."

Mrs. Wunderlich bounds over to the coffee table, stops, scans the magazines. No *People,* no *Vanity Fair,* no *InStyle.* She notices the flowers. She wonders if it is true that florists have deals with funeral homes and graveyards, that they recycle flowers grieving families leave behind. She sits, crossing her legs at the ankle. Her eyes fall on the other woman in the waiting area. She thinks the woman is what is called "put together." She thinks the woman would look ten years younger if Louis Licari colored her hair.

At ten-fifteen, a young man in a crisp white shirt pushes open a glass door.

"Mrs. Vogel?" he says.

The tall woman clicks her pen. She rolls the magazine section and is tucking it in her purse when the man says, "Mrs. Wunderlich?" The woman in the velvet flats looks up.

"I'm Jonathan Oliphant." The young man nods. "Glad you could make it."

The women stare at each other.

Mrs. Wunderlich says, "You want to see us both?"

Mrs. Vogel frowns.

Mr. Oliphant taps his tie. "If you'll follow me, please."

They trail him past secretaries in cubicles to an office at the end of the hall. The walls are thick with law books. Mrs. Vogel's youngest son, David, has told her all he really learned in law school was where to look things up.

Mr. Oliphant stands behind his desk. He extends a palm. "Please," he gestures. The women sit.

"Mrs. Vogel, Mrs. Wunderlich, first of all, I'd like to thank you both for making the time to come this morning. As you know from my letter, I represent the estate of the late Roberta Heumann Bloom."

There is a sharp intake of breath. The lawyer glances at Mrs. Wunderlich and continues. "Mrs. Bloom had great confidence in both of you."

Mrs. Wunderlich sniffs. "Sorry." She rummages in her bag.

The lawyer opens and closes desk drawers but no tissues are forthcoming. In the spirit of moving things along, Mrs. Vogel produces a fresh hankie. She is grateful it is not a monogrammed one. Bidding the hankie a silent goodbye, she passes it to Mrs. Wunderlich.

"Thank you," Mrs. Wunderlich says.

Mr. Oliphant begins: "Do you remember, each of you, when Mrs. Bloom was ill, being asked to sign a bank-vault card?"

"Yes," Mrs. Vogel responds. "I remember. For access to her safety-deposit box."

He slides an envelope across his desk. It is pale blue and perfectly square. Both women recognize their friend's stationery.

"This envelope contains the key to that vault and a letter," Mr. Oliphant continues. "I have no idea what is in the vault or what Mrs. Bloom wrote."

Mrs. Vogel reaches for the envelope. She turns it over. It is sealed with duct tape. Both women smile. Their friend had faith in duct tape. She used it to repair hems and mask blinking LED displays on TVs and clocks. It kept AA batteries in place when she lost the little door on her Walkman. Once she kept a square on her finger for a week and it cured a wart.

"One more thing," the lawyer adds. "Mrs. Bloom requested that you read the letter here, in my presence."

Mrs. Wunderlich buries her face in Mrs. Vogel's hankie. Mrs. Vogel strips the duct tape and pulls out the letter. A key with a numbered tag clatters to the desk. Mrs. Vogel clears her throat.

"Dearest Alice and Nanny," she reads aloud, "Dearest Nanny and Alice, Dear Dearest Friends in No Particular Order, Please go now to the Chase on Fifty-eighth and Madison. Open the box together. You'll know what to do. Love you to pieces."

Mrs. Wunderlich blows her nose.

Mrs. Vogel snatches the key and slips it in her purse.

"My first name is Alice," Alice Vogel offers as they head for the bank. It is Wednesday, matinee day, and already traffic is heavier than usual.

"I'm Nanny," Nanny Wunderlich replies.

"How did you know Roberta?" Alice asks.

"We met in grad school. Both of us were pregnant. We did La Perla, I mean La Bamba, I mean *Lamaze* together." Nanny shakes her head with every wrong name as if she can rattle out the right one. "Our daughters were born twelve days apart."

"Are you a marriage-and-family therapist as well?" Alice asks.

"My specialty was early childhood. And you? How did you know Bobbie?"

"Our mothers were friends. Roberta's mother was my godmother. My mother was Roberta's."

"So you've known her forever," Nanny says.

"Since utero."

The light changes. A bike messenger swerves, barely missing them. They make their way across the street.

"I was her best friend," Alice resumes.

"You were her oldest friend," Nanny corrects. "Interesting we've never met."

Alice purses her lips. "Roberta didn't care to mix people. Surely you knew that. Except at those parties."

"Yeah." Nanny nods. "Right. A one-on-one kind of girl."

Nanny glances sideways at Alice. She wonders if this is the friend of Bobbie's who got an STD from her husband. No, that was Linda "Largemouth" Bassin. The one whose daughter wasn't her husband's? No, that was her college roommate, Janie Something. Was this the one who was boffing her son's science teacher? Nanny recalls a woman off in a corner at birthday parties, sipping coffee. A well-dressed woman with boys in blue blazers.

"I know you," Nanny says. "I'm pretty sure. Yeah. From Betsy's birthday parties. You have boys?"

"I have two sons. Yes." Alice recalls the loud blur of Betsy's endless birthdays. She looks at Nanny and remembers a frenetic woman, quite pretty, by Roberta's side. Every year the woman wore Farmer Brown overalls and helped Roberta settle the children for Mr. Shazam! or Buzzy the Clown. "You're starting to look somewhat familiar too," Alice adds.

They stop to look in the window of a store that sells place mats, netsukes, and vases out of frosted glass.

It occurs to Alice this might be the friend of Roberta's whose husband went to country-club jail for insider trading. Or the one who was caught having sex in a dressing room at Burberry's. Perhaps this is the friend whose husband came out of Central Park and had a heart attack on the sidewalk, the one whose husband died in her arms.

"I think I remember you from the Valentine parties," Alice says as they resume walking. "Were you at Roberta's Valentine's Day parties?"

"You were too?" Nanny says.

"I never cared for theme parties," Alice says. "The implication is: Alas, dear guests. You're simply not stimulating enough."

"You're kidding, right?" Nanny says. "Those parties were a blast."

"I prefer entertaining in a restaurant. Six for dinner. A round table."

"I could feed forty for what that costs in New York," Nanny says. "You throw parties in restaurants?"

"Little dinners in restaurants. To reciprocate for other people's little dinners in restaurants."

"After my husband died," Nanny says, "I stopped going to parties. Cold-turkey. Bobbie's. Everybody's."

"How odd," Alice replies. "I'd imagine that's precisely when one should go."

"You know what? In a coupled world, parties are pure torture."

"Parties with friends?"

"The pits," Nanny says. "Wives worry you're trolling, that every husband's a live one. People feel like saints just for talking to you, mercy conversations. I hate being single around married people. Widowhood, you might as well live in India. It's a pariah subculture."

This must be the one whose husband died on the sidewalk, Alice thinks.

"Being a widow," Nanny continues, "gives people you hardly know permission to swim up to you and say, 'When are you selling the apartment?' or 'Do you miss sex?' or 'What's your number? My seventy-nine-year-old cousin just had a bypass.' "

"How brutal," Alice says. She checks her watch. She does it scratching her wrist to make it appear she is merely scratching her wrist.

The light turns green. "That lawyer was so young," Nanny says, stepping off the curb.

"Doctors, policemen, firefighters. They're babies now."

"Oh look," Nanny says. "There's a butterfly on your sleeve."

Alice stops. *"Polygonia interrogationis,"* she says.

"What?"

"A question mark butterfly. See the angular notched forewings?"

"A butterfly in November?"

"Global warming," Alice says. "We're seeing *Polygonia* year-round now." She blows it off her arm.

"How come you know so much about bugs?"

"My eldest was an amateur entomologist."

"Funny what you get to be an expert on from your kids. Ask me anything, anything at all, about gypsy punk."

They turn right. "There's the Plaza Theatre." Nanny points straight ahead. "Bobbie and I loved going to the early show."

"You went to movies during the day?"

"That's the best time. No lines. You come out, the shank of the day's ahead of you. You get popcorn for lunch plus a good movie."

"Well." Alice squares her shoulders. "Roberta and I, we did other things." She lengthens her stride. "Roberta and I, we preferred theater."

"Last year," Nanny continues, "when she was bald, she used to tell the ticket guy she was a senior. She'd get in for seven dollars instead of ten-fifty."

"Roberta was fifty-eight."

"She called it, 'The sole advantage of chemo.' "

"Roberta and I did other things," Alice says again. "We jogged up Riverside Drive every morning."

"You're the running pal?"

"And," Alice continues, "our mothers' birthdays were celebrated at a joint luncheon until Aunt Edith died."

"I knew Mrs. Heumann too," Nanny says. "We'd have lunch together too. Though not with my mother. My mother died when I was seventeen."

"How terrible," Alice says. "She must have been young."

"I'm twenty-one years older now than she was then."

"Roberta made me promise to take Betsy for her wedding gown," Alice says.

"She made me promise too," Nanny says.

Alice checks her watch again. "Mind picking up the pace? I'm awfully sorry but I've got to get to work."

Nanny notices the bracelet. "So you got the other one."

The women hold their arms out and match wrists while they wait for the light.

ALLERGIC TO FISH
WEARING CONTACT LENSES

"You know, a bit of punctuation would have gone a long way toward clarity," Alice says.

"Then it wouldn't have been funny."

"But two medical-alert bracelets?"

"What if one arm got blown off?" Nanny asks.

"How Roberta."

"I miss her more than I can say," Nanny says.

Alice nods. "I do too."

"Hey, see that guy?" Nanny points to a man on the northeast corner selling handbags. "Bobbie thought he had the best knock-offs in the city. Better than Canal Street. Faux Fendi, faux Bottega. Spitting distance from Fendi and Bottega. How do they get away with it?"

"They're blatantly fake. That's how. I can see it from here."

"Really?"

"I have to. It's my job."

"What do you do? Some special kind of police work?"

"I own Luba."

Luba. Nanny can picture the sign. *"Luba"* in deep-pink script on a beige background. "The secondhand store on Madison?"

Alice frowns. "The preowned boutique."

"Do you get your clothes there?" Nanny asks.

"Please."

Nanny shrugs. "Seems like a no-brainer."

"How would my customers trust me? How would they know I wasn't setting prices in my own favor? Think about it."

"When I don't want my stuff anymore, I give it to the cleaning lady."

They cross in silence.

"So anyway," Nanny tries to revive the conversation, "I stopped being a therapist after my husband died."

She waits for Alice to ask what she currently does. Finally Nanny says, "Now I'm a real-estate broker." She waits for the usual questions.

Alice remains silent.

"Want a Tic Tac?"

"I never eat between meals."

"Bobbie loved wintergreen." Nanny raises her chin and shakes a flurry into her mouth.

A gust of wind blows a blue plastic bag over Nanny's ankle. Alice steps back as Nanny stomps it off. It cartwheels north and snags the fetlock of a carriage horse. The horse looks as if he is wearing one blue gaiter.

At the bank Alice says, "Here we are."

Together they push through the doors.

"So what do you think's in the vault?" Nanny asks.

"I can't imagine."

"Think it's money?" she persists.

"Any response to that," Alice says, "is reckless speculation."

. . .

Shoulder to shoulder they stand in front of a locked glass door. A woman sitting behind a desk laughs into a phone. She plays with her hair, twisting shiny black ringlets around her index finger.

Alice leans on the entry button. The woman looks up. Her eyes widen as if Nanny and Alice are old friends dropping by. She continues her conversation.

"This is unacceptable behavior," Alice says.

"She's just a kid."

"That's a personal call on company time. I've got an eleven-thirty appointment and she's ignoring us."

"Lighten up," Nanny mutters.

"What?"

"Right." Nanny stares straight ahead.

Alice buzzes staccato. The woman cups her hand over the mouthpiece. She whispers into the phone then hangs up. Smiling, she buzzes Nanny and Alice in.

"Good morning, ladies!"

Alice slaps the key case on the desk. "Box 714."

"Name?" the woman rises from her chair.

"Vogel. Alice Vogel."

"Fogel?"

"Vogel."

"Could you spell that, please?"

Alice glances at the woman's name tag. She commits "Tina Gurry" to memory.

"V as in Venal. O as in Obstreperous. G as in Ghastly. E as in Egregious. L as in Lackluster or Lackadaisical or Ludicrous. Or Laughable or Lice."

Ms. Gurry studies Alice like a bird at a wormhole. She raises her right hand and jounces a six-inch ring crammed with skinny, oddly shaped keys. She jiggles them in Alice's face like bait then flips through a card file. "I don't seem to have a V-O-G-E-L," she sighs.

"Could I trouble you to check under my name?" Nanny says. "Wunderlich, with a U?"

Ms. Gurry locates the W tab. She plucks a card. "Here we are, Mrs. Wunderlich. Let's see. There is a notation. It says here you both must sign in together, Mrs. Wunderlich and Mrs. Beagle."

She passes Nanny her pen. When both women have signed in, Ms. Gurry compares the signatures. With grave attention to task, she rips the scraps into confetti and snows them over a wastebasket.

"Follow me, please," she says.

Nanny worries. She has read newspaper stories about old people who go to their safety-deposit boxes, open them, and all the diamonds smuggled out, sewn into the lining of coats, or swallowed—were gone. What if there is nothing in the box? Contents of a vault can't be proved.

Ms. Gurry leads them past a round steel door. It measures two feet thick and is covered with gears and gauges like a prop from a Batman movie.

They step into a long narrow room lined floor to ceiling with built-in metal boxes. The boxes are dull green and come in five sizes, from barely big enough for a paperback book to roomy enough for the Yellow Pages. Ms. Gurry walks slowly, scanning up and down, studying numbers.

"Ah!" She stops. "Here we are!"

It is a small one by the floor. Alice thinks it must be horrible to have the kind of job where you have to stoop for people. On the other hand, Ms. Gurry gets to dress up every day like a banker. She is entrusted to check signatures. Ms. Gurry can choose to buzz or not buzz. She has a Chase health plan.

The face of the box presents horizontal slots for two keys. Ms. Gurry tries several on her ring. When satisfied, she inserts the key Alice gave her into the other hole. She twists both to the right. A welcome click is followed by a long metal scrape. The box pulls out of the wall like a corpse on a slab.

Ms. Gurry lays it in Nanny's outstretched hands. The women follow her back to the waiting area.

"Which room would you like?" She directs her question to Nanny.

Both are white. Both are windowless. Both have two chairs and a Formica ledge that serves as a desk.

It occurs to Alice one could have a tryst in these rooms. For the price of a three by eighteen inch safe-deposit box, one could have a locked room in midtown every day during banking hours.

"What is the difference between the rooms?" she asks.

"They're identical," Ms. Gurry says.

"We'll take this one." Nanny enters the room on the left. Alice follows, closing the door.

They pull up swivel chairs. Except for the hum of the fluorescent light, the room is still. An old-fashioned adding machine with a paper roll sits on the ledge beside a gnawed Mongol pencil.

They stare at the box.

"Why would she do this?"

"We'll know in a minute," Alice says.

"Think it's a diary?"

"Whatever it is, we know one thing."

"What?" Nanny asks.

"Roberta chose *us* to see the contents."

Nanny rolls her chair closer to the ledge. "Want to open it together?"

"As in, we both put our hands on it and say one-two-three?"

"Shoot you for it," Nanny offers, raising a fist. "Evens!"

"Oh really." Alice says. "You may have the honor."

"The last person to see what was in here was Bobbie." Nanny's voice wobbles. "You know what that means?"

"Frankly no," Alice says.

"Her breath is in this box."

Alice grows impatient. She presses her finger beneath the metal latch and flips it.

Both women lean in.

"Here goes something," Nanny says.

She raises the lid.

4 · Nanny Reads

Forget the counter. I don't need some busybody snooping over my shoulder. I park myself in a booth.

Why did Bobbie want Ice Maiden to come with me?

"I'd like a bowl of chicken-noodle soup."

The waiter stands there.

"And a toasted English."

He's not moving.

"And a coffee. Black. Okay?"

He turns on his heel. Forty-five minutes till the Glogowers. I take out the letter:

Thursday, August 1—
My dearest, my love, my heart–

August 1 when? What year?

I'm writing you on the very eve of one of the Great Battles of the Civil War,

Why was he writing about the Civil War?

the Rebs all geared up to shell Fort Sumter and Lincoln pondering deeply beneath the unfinished Iron Dome of the Capitol Building.

Were they into antebellum sex? Corsets and buggy whips?

At such moments any soldier who Calls Himself a Man pauses amid the hustle and anxieties of Imminent Conflict to pen a heart-felt note to his Girl.

Ay caramba.

You'll be getting this, I hope, a day or two before I hold you in my arms again.

"Again." It was a thing?

25

Your letter was so beautiful and our visit so uncluttered. I remember on the first day how all I had to do was touch you. It is lovely to watch your face then. There is no time when you are more beautiful.

Freddy looked like a troll when he came.

I pray someday I can wake up beside you, kiss you awake, make breakfast for you,

I'll give that five minutes. Tops.

then after work, a walk before dinner, or maybe make love in late-summer dusk, and spend the evening reading my book to you, stroking and kissing.

". . . my book . . . ?" A book he wrote? A book he owned?

You're what I've always hoped for, someone who loves to give pleasure as much as receive it. That's the great secret, the rare virtue. You are innately loving.

You got it.

And generally wonderful.

In spades.

Do you know that when I hear you say my name I feel it all over my body? I want everything you have to spare for me. I want you, want you, want you.

I get it, get it, get it.

You've taught me what I never knew I was capable of.

All I knew was what she wanted me to know.

With you I can be as extravagant as I like. Mind, you'll always outdo me.

"Mind." Southern.

Will you wear that lacy frou-frou again, the one with the pink ribbons up the front?

We got those at Loehmann's!

I consider it my heavenly mandate to unlace them. Slowly. Perhaps with my teeth.

Did Jack know? Betsy?

I worry about myself if I lose you, but I worry about you too. Who will tell you how lovely you are?

"Lovely" wasn't in Fred's vocabulary either.

Who will kiss your bracelets? Your montes?

Montes? What the hell is a montes? Do I have one?

There is so much to remember, but right now on my mind is you singing to me in the car, your little-girl voice,

Love is deaf. She sang like Betty Boop.

your pleasure in singing for me. You astonish me. I don't think we've ever made love without an experience that was new to both of us.

Yeah. Well. Give it time. Which is not to say, Freddypie, that it wasn't very heaven.

And there are so many beans left to put in the jar, every one of them a rare and exquisite time together.

Beans in the jar. I remember that. If you put a bean in a jar every time you made love the first year, and you took a bean out every time you made love after that, ten years later there would still be beans in the jar.

In five days, I see you again. I planted a kiss on a critical place in your panties. Could you tell?

It would kill Jack seeing this.

My life feels illuminated. I am alive in every corner of my being. I cherish you. Every minute without you contains an emptiness. I am honored by your feelings toward me. I love you far beyond words. I can only really spell it out with my lips.

Beats a ballpoint.

Here you are, the woman I've always dreamed about, here you are at last. I want you. My heart is bursting. All my love, all of it. You're my sweetheart, my only sweetheart. I really do love you, you see.

Who the hell were you, Bobbie Bloom?

5 · Alice Deciphers

Well, well, well. A posthumous surprise. To two old friends. Why, Roberta dear? Why both of us? Above all, why now?

The bus driver pulls tight to the curb. He raises a metal bar and proceeds down the aisle. At the rear door he unlocks the disabled lift. It hums. I settle back, open my bag, and retrieve the Xerox.

Thursday, August 1—
My dearest, my love, my heart–
I'm writing you on the very eve of one of the Great Battles of the Civil War,
Clearly a Southerner. The reference point for everything.
the Rebs all geared up to shell Fort Sumter and Lincoln pondering deeply beneath the unfinished Iron Dome of the Capitol Building. At such moments any soldier who Calls Himself a Man pauses amid the hustle and anxieties of Imminent Conflict to pen a heart-felt note to his Girl.
Are you laughing from above, Roberta dear? I am not aching to have this information. You in particular would have known that.
You'll be getting this, I hope, a day or two before I hold you in my arms again. Your letter was so beautiful and our visit so unclut-tered. I remember on the first day how all I had to do was touch you.
Now I understand. You wanted me to know I was not alone. This letter is a gift. Then why include that woman? Did she have a lover too?
It is lovely to watch your face then. There is no time when you are more beautiful.

28

I pray someday I can wake up beside you, kiss you awake, make breakfast for you,

I never awakened beside Mr. Wald. Why would I have wanted to.

then after work, a walk before dinner, or maybe make love in late-summer dusk, and spend the evening reading my book to you,

Perhaps he read Yeats to her.

stroking and kissing.

You're what I've always hoped for, someone who loves to give pleasure as much as receive it.

If I'd never met Mr. Wald, I would still believe sex was pressure rasping to a finish line.

That's the great secret, the rare virtue. You are innately loving. And generally wonderful. Do you know that when I hear you say my name I feel it all over my body? I want everything you have to spare for me. I want you, want you, want you.

You've taught me what I never knew I was capable of.

Thank you, Mr. Wald, for being a most excellent teacher.

With you I can be as extravagant as I like. Mind, you'll always outdo me.

Should I let Charles read this? A man who believes foreplay means playing with your forearm? If you tell a lover, "I like when you run the tip of your tongue along the curve of my upper lip," he will never forget it, but he'll be careful not to overuse it, not do it every time so it becomes routine and predictable. If suggested to Charles, no matter how gently couched, he'd pout, "You don't like the way I kiss?"

But. If you said to a lover, "I like when you run your tongue on the curve of my upper lip," he would find ten ways to run his tongue there, using muscles you didn't know the tongue had. He would know it was so intense, something had to come before it and around it, it needed to be broken off and started again. He would know everything that needed to be known by your breath, the cant of your hips.

To My Dearest Friends

Will you wear that lacy frou-frou again, the one with the pink ribbons up the front? I consider it my heavenly mandate to unlace them. Slowly. Perhaps with my teeth.

So much for Hanes.

I worry about myself if I lose you, but I worry about you too. Who will tell you how lovely you are? Who will kiss your bracelets? Your montes?

It's never over. Never.

There is so much to remember, but right now on my mind is you singing to me in the car, your little-girl voice,

Roberta won the lead in camp every year.

your pleasure in singing for me. You astonish me. I don't think we've ever made love without an experience that was new to both of us. And there are so many

What does this say? This handwriting is impossible. So many what? So many bums? Burns? Seams? Is that a B? An S? So many burns hate topic under sir? So many seams sent hotel inner jam? Bums soft to plot inner war? Soft? Safe? So many bums safe to plot inner war? That must be it. Some arcane Civil War reference to itinerant military strategists. A lovers' code?

And there are so many bums safe to plot inner war, every one of them a rare and exquisite time together.

In five days, I see you again. I planted a kiss on a critical place in your panties.

Oh.

Could you tell?

My life feels illuminated. I am alive in every corner of my being. I cherish you. Every minute without you contains an emptiness. I am honored by your feelings toward me. I love you far beyond words. I can only really spell it out with my lips. Here you are, the woman I've always dreamed about, here you are at last. I want you. My heart is bursting. All my love, all of it. You're my sweetheart, my only sweetheart. I really do love you, you see.

Brava, Roberta. You lunatic.

6 · Nanny Wonders

I fish out my Metrocard and hop the Lex. What was she thinking? All the planning that went into it. And for what?

I'll be early for the Glogowers. Better an hour early than one minute late. Late, you start out apologizing. Worse, you do the L.A. thing where you *don't* apologize. You give the client you've kept waiting a list of all the critical things you were doing. Then your client's supposed to think: *Aren't I lucky? This wildly busy person made time for me.*

I could care less waiting for clients, long as it doesn't make me late for my next appointment. I can go home, run errands. There are two libraries in Carnegie Hill, seven museums. Used to be eight, till the ICP was sold. Seventeen point two, the photography center went for. When word got out, all brokers could say was "Seventeen point two million! That's insane!" Next month they were gasping, "Do you believe? He got that for only seventeen two?"

If you have trouble waiting, find another calling. Showings end early. Some people whiz through an eight in three minutes. They may not know what they want but they're sure what they don't. Others prowl, sidling into rooms, orienting themselves, trying to find the kitchen yet again as if they've beamed down from Mars. They clutch the floor plan, checking how the Sheraton sideboard will work. They make a career out of it, turning on every faucet, flushing every toilet. They light matches by the windows to see if the flame sputters. "How old are the air conditioners?" "When was the refrigerator replaced?" "What are the restrictions re moving non–weight-bearing walls?" They actually say "re." On the other hand, these are people willing to enslave themselves to a thirty-year flexible mortgage. Young couples on Medicare before it's paid off.

Why didn't Bobbie tell us what to do? How are we supposed to know?

Poor Glogowers. Will they like this place? Six months they've been looking. A baby on the way. At least I got to stage the place. Some sellers, it's tough to convince putting in five will get them another fifty. Still, I got to paint the brown bedroom yellow and rewire the closets so the light pops on when you open the door. The Wow Factor. Gives buyers permission to believe the rest of the apartment is state-of-the-art too.

East Seventy-ninth Street to East Ninety-eighth, Park to Fifth, that's my turf, prime New York real estate. Miracle is, I still live on Ninety-sixth and Madison. Despite Fred's Incredible Shrinking TIAA-CREF, I haven't lost my home. Not yet. I've changed careers, given up a steady income, but I was more than ready. Thirty-one years of toddlers crying eight hours nonstop. Babies catching depression. And the new thing: parents frothing to litigate if you refuse to write a letter saying "the emotional health of Bradley will be at risk if forced to leave your school." Time for something else and being a broker uses everything I've learned about people. Eventually I'll make loot. I have to be patient. I'm low woman on the totem pole. No, I'm the part of the totem pole buried underground. I get the wreck, the client from hell, the tough sell to the board. The divorcée with bad plastic surgery and nine cats. I am better at one thing than anybody. Difficult people. If I'm not a therapist anymore technically, I'm doing what I always did. Assessments. Ways out of chaos.

I plop on the couch. This particular New York lobby configuration I call "The Ersatz Living Room." A rug with a sofa, two chairs, and a coffee table in a cavernous prewar hall, like tea is about to be served. In front of each doctor's entrance, a gray metal box with a throbbing red caduceus awaits a messenger. Their contents—vials of dark blood, slivers of suspicious tissue, blebs and moles—all headed for New York's intrepid pathologists. That's a job, carrying that box, carrying the inevitable. Fate in a box.

And what's a good fate? Freddy's? So fast, no time to suffer, no knowledge you're dying? Dead at fifty-six? Well it wasn't good for me. Sorry. Uh-uh. Not good at all. Better than Bobbie's maybe, with your husband and child watching you waste, wishing it was over because they love you too much to see you suffer, then wishing they could unwish that. Bad news and good news snarled like a rat's nest, impossible to tease apart. Healthy friends struggling to intuit what you want them to do. Be cheery? Neutral? Glum? Be hopeful? Mournful? Wait to be called? Call and risk intruding? Whatever you were, the last thing you could be was authentic. And by not being able to be yourself, you knew you were doing damage. If love could cure, Bobbie and I would be meeting Flora and Betsy for dinner. We'd be in the lobby of the Paris Theatre arguing whether fake butter on popcorn shortens your life.

Tragic. Here I am, fifty-nine, still young. In ways that count, I'm in my prime. But I won't get to be old with my closest friend. Or my husband. A whole part of my life will never take place. Without Fred, there's no one I can discuss Flora with risk-free, her interest purely at heart. How can it be, that just when you're old enough to appreciate your husband, he's old enough to die? Why doesn't anybody tell you what to expect? Why isn't Getting Older taught in school? Learning to make cocoa in Home Ec—"Now, girls, bend your knees until you're eye-level with the red line on your Pyrex cup!"—that was more important? Teach Marriage. Teach Raising a Daughter followed by Losing a Mate. Wouldn't that be more valuable than Geometry? What good is a cosine now? Why did I have to learn things that can't be remembered? Teach Life. One high-school semester. Devote the last week to Aging. Who would believe it? A roomful of hormonally charged seventeen-year-olds? They'd laugh their randy heads off. It's like every person over fifty belongs to the Secret Aging Club, and no one wants you to know that "long in the tooth" isn't a metaphor. Or why people say, "I'm sorry. I don't eat anything with seeds."

What next? For the last three years, the internist's been asking, "Which joint hurts most?" Then he asks, "How many times do you get up at night to tinkle?" Frankly, Dr. Wishniak, I don't and I'm not crazy about the word "tinkle" either. What happened to terms like "void" and "urinate"? No joints hurt and I urinate maybe twice a day. Thanks for the sneak decrepitude preview, doc. I can hear you saying it, Fred: "Easy come. Hard go."

Oh no. Am I turning into your mother? Am I Ida Finkel Wunderlich, talking to her dead husband? This has got to stop, Freddy. I'm talking more to you now than when you were alive.

Did Jack know? Did Bobbie want me to tell him? Why have that grump come too?

The Glogowers are seven minutes late. I put on my headphones and find NPR. A woman is saying, ". . . new Social Security plan. I don't understand, Mr. President. How will your proposal help me?"

How lucky. I don't get this new Social Security thing at all.

"Thank you for asking that question," the President responds. "That's a fine question. Let me explain. Because the, all which is on the table begins to address the big cost drivers. There's a series of parts of the formula that are being considered. For example, how benefits are calculated, for example, is on the table. And when you couple that, those different cost drivers, changing those with personal accounts, the idea is to get what has been promised more likely to be, or closer delivered to that which has been promised. You get it now? Look, there's a series of things like, for example, benefits are calculated based upon the increase of wages, as opposed to the increase of prices. There is a reform that would help solve the red if that were put into effect. In other words, it will help on the red."

·   ·   ·

Tom enters The Ersatz Living Room. "I'm getting coffee, Mrs. Wunderlich. Want some?"

I'm coffeed out. One more cup, I'll be a coffee witch. I hand him a ten. "A small black, please. Keep the change."

I make sure doormen in buildings I show are happy to see me. They make it easy. This matters. You had a name for it, Freddy. The Favor Bank. Be nice to somebody, they'll owe you. A veteran doorman's package with benefits, that's $120,000 easy. Tom makes more than I do. Why am I tipping him? I should be getting Tom coffee, keeping *his* change. Tom has more disposable income than I do, but I live around the corner and he takes two subways to Queens. Welcome to the New York Economic Funhouse.

How come Bobbie didn't tell me while she was alive? Why now? And that pissy friend of hers. Think I'll file her card under "B."

I reach for the letter, and the Glogowers fly into the lobby. Meredith explodes apologies. I ready my face into my You Are My Favorite Clients look. Steven Glogower hangs back, avoiding eye contact.

We wait in front of the elevator door. Our images warp in the polished brass. The Glogowers are miserable. The Glogowers are six months pregnant in a postwar studio east of Third. The Lemon Wedge Building, I call it, because of its strangely slapped-on terraces. Meredith needs to move. Steve is scared. There's been a decline in consumer confidence, a budding skepticism. Meredith will do whatever it takes to make the kind of home she believes with her heart is in their best interest. Fear gnaws Steve's bones. It is my job to make all parties happy. In the best of all possible worlds, the seller will be bowled over by the selling price and the Glogowers will think they got a deal. It could happen.

7 · Alice Ruminates

I can see it from the corner, purring by the curb. The Vandervoort limo. Am I late? No, it is eleven-twenty. Mrs. Vandervoort is early.

I walk to Luba, eyes straight ahead. It would not do for Mrs. Vandervoort to know I know she is anxious. It would not do to acknowledge she is waiting for me. Mrs. Vandervoort and her ilk are out nightly. They are in the Style section Sunday and the society pages of glossy magazines sent free to select East Side addresses. These magazines are made up entirely of jewelry ads and snapshots of women at galas wearing that jewelry. Society ladies cannot be seen in the same dress twice. Mrs. Vandervoort consigns a Valentino to Luba. A friend of hers comes in and buys the Valentino. A friend of Mrs. Vandervoort's consigns a Lanvin. Mrs. Vandervoort discovers that one. On occasion Mrs. Vander-voort consigns a dress she bought from me I sell yet again. Praise heaven for charity dinners and Chanel.

I remove the padlock and raise the security gate. My kingdom, my mother's and grandmother's before me. I unlock the door and flick on the light. My empire. Daily, invariably, I ruminate: What if I hadn't married Charles? What if I hadn't had Jason right away? What if I'd taken my orals for "The Influence of the Occult Aes-thetic of William Butler Yeats on Virginia Woolf's *The Waves*"? What if?

I busy myself behind the Louis XIV desk where financial trans-actions quietly take place. Mrs. Vandervoort's driver steps out of the limo. He opens her door and offers a forearm. Once she is safely encurbed, he retrieves a Vuitton garment bag from the front seat.

I treat my customers as if they are brilliant and chic for shopping Luba, and they are. Luba garments hang in impeccable condition. They are crisp. With the exception of Le Coin du Vintage, a Luba garment is rarely more than a year old. Instead of the Schiaparellis, Mainbochers, and Nettie Rosensteins their grandmothers cherished, instead of the Claire McCardells, Pauline Trigères and Nina Riccis their mothers coveted, today's society ladies seek Armani evening gowns reduced to fifteen hundred dollars. They load up on Oscars, Veras, and Yves. They scan Le Coin and pluck a Beene or Blass. A Balmain, a Brooks.

Women shop Luba because they trust my taste. They come confident I will steer them to something breathtaking. I know my customers. I know my stock. Like my grandmother, like my mother, I have total garment-recall. This is essential in my métier.

And my patrons rest assured: At Luba there are no stains, no shiny patches. No pulled threads or split seams. Everything hangs in privileged perfection on a padded ecru *peau-de-soie* hanger. Price tags are affixed with satin ribbons and tiny gold safety pins, never nasty plastic wires. Accounts are meticulously kept. Dressing rooms are individual, each with its own cheval mirror. Luba's floor is layered with Moroccan rugs. The walls and ceiling are an upholstered souk of pink and beige stripes. Every piece of clothing is handled as if it were destined for the Costume Institute at the Metropolitan Museum, and hot green tea is served on a chased silver tray. So it is. So it has always been. Above all, and there is no way to overstate the importance, no way to put it delicately, what sets us apart is, Luba is without any trace whatsoever of Eau de Corps, the telltale consignment-shop smell, the smell that broadcasts the word we at Luba never use: *used.*

And you, Roberta, were one of my best customers. And you did not try to insinuate a discount despite our friendship. Did you wear those flirty Moschino suits? That rubber Versace? The Yoshiki Hishinuma you bought because you said it looked like a car crash? I did not see you in them. Not once. Were you buying them to be generous to me? Oh Roberta dear, what would you like me to do with your unwanted information?

Mrs. Vandervoort latches on to her driver. They approach the door. Mrs. Vandervoort stops, checks the window. I use the same dressmaker dummy Mother and Grand-mère used. It actually is my grandmother Luba Fertig Fargotstein, her headless, legless torso in mellow canvas stretched tight over wood and wire. Fabricated in Paris by Poiret's mannequin-maker prior to World War I, Luba rolls on her filigree cast-iron base as smoothly as if she were skating at Rockefeller Center. I personally change her every month. I select what Luba presents to the world. Today she is wearing a vintage Maggy Rouff Little Brown Wren dress, the dress the quiet lady at the table who gets all the men wears. The fabric is a humble sheer wool the color of a field mouse. The cut, however, is exquisite, the portrait collar designed to frame a face, to make a face the star.

Mrs. Vandervoort's chauffeur waits while she studies the Rouff. It would not be good for her. She is too old to rely on her face. Her attraction now is relegated to personal grooming and the disciplined art of impeccable maintenance. It is in the perfecting of what remains, the flawless manicure, the creamed and scented décolletage. Shoes with polished soles. Moneyed hair. If she insists on trying the dress, I will, of course, oblige. If she asks me how she looks in the Rouff, I will be honest. I will, however, take into consideration how I see Mrs. Vandervoort feels in the dress, how Mrs. Vandervoort sees herself, the power of the transformative unknown.

Mrs. Vandervoort's driver presses the bell. I look up, feigning surprise. He transfers the Vuitton, draping it over Mrs. Vandervoort's newly impatient arm. She is wearing her trademark fly-eye sunglasses with rose lenses. If she took them off, no one would know she was Mrs. Vandervoort consigning at Luba. But since she very much is Mrs. Vandervoort, I do not buzz her in. I go to the door and open it as if she is a most welcome guest in my home and say, "Mrs. Vandervoort! How lovely to see you! Please! Allow me to take that! Tea?"

8 · A Saucy Dog Laps His Own Tail

Not in the handbag.

Not by the mail.

Not on the chair.

Back to the handbag.

This time dump the handbag.

How many hours of a life could you get back if the first time you looked for something you did it so you didn't need to look again? You never had this trouble, Freddy. People who grow up wearing glasses don't. You had one pair. When you took them off to give a lecture, you tucked them in your bulletproof case on that dainty blue cloth, a cloth so soft it could be a baby's Blankie, Zummie, or Ah-Ah. That case molded your pocket. When you came home after classes, it went on the dresser alongside your wallet, keys, change. Thunk, slap, clink, jangle, a tidy Freddy ritual. If you grow up needing glasses, you imprint keeping track of them.

Where are they? How many pairs have I gone through this year? Green pair sat on yesterday. Plaid ones from the Dollar Store forgotten in jeans, warped in dryer. Popped lenses, missing screws. The pair that slid into boiling rigatoni.

Pocket.

Let's see. . . . How did I get on the mailing list of a catalog with dildos? What have I done to generate the interest of Harry and David? Who cares? I'm so happy to be home, I could fall on my knees and kiss the quarter-sawn oak.

The Glogowers hated the apartment. Who could blame them. The Kleckners loved the apartment. Who could blame them.

The phone is blinking. Five new messages.

"Hello? This is Mercedes Flynn? I was wondering if I could see
12B at 1148 again? How's tomorrow morning? Eight-fifteen? I'm
having second thoughts about the twelfth floor? Fire ladders only
go up to eight, and . . ."

BEEP!

"Mrs. Wunderlich? This is Beatrice Sambaba from Sparkle. My
girls can't clean the Hahn apartment. Not based on our usual terms.
Did you see what was in that apartment, Mrs. Wunderlich? Did
you notice the wall behind the lavatory? And those mattresses?
And what was that in the sink, Mrs. Wunderlich? My God. I feel
certain you will understand, Mrs. Wunderlich. You can't expect my
girls to go in there. This is not a routine job, no, no. You can leave
a log in water long as you like. It will never be a crocodile."

Log? Crocodile?

BEEP!

"Hello. This is Plate City. If you have a plate missing from your
dinner service, chances are we can replace it. Plate City has over
one million . . ."

BEEP!

"It's Jeanette, Nanny. Give me a call. Something up your way."

BEEP!

"Hey, Mom. It's meeeeeeee!"

I dial Flora at the magazine. Flora, my Floradora Girl. Floradorable. Even her voice on the answering machine makes for
thudding feelings.

"Flora Wunderlich," she answers.

"Hi, sweetheart!"

"Ma! I've got two free tickets for the Knicks Monday. Wanna
go?"

I'm deeply touched. I'm profoundly moved, even though this
means Flora has gone through her list of friends and drawn a
blank. Still, it means my very beautiful, very wonderful, brilliant,
amazing, still-unmarried daughter doesn't mind spending time
with me. Truth be told, no, I don't want to go to the Knicks, even

with Floradorable. I don't want to take two subways to Thirty-
fourth after work, then forge beery crowds to watch grown men
fling sweat over a ball.

"Sure," I say.

I dial Jeanette at the office. The apartment she wants me to
show is on Ninety-seventh and Fifth. Great building. A classic six.
Why is she giving it to me? What's the catch?

"Is it ours?" I ask.

"A co-broke," Jeannette answers.

Right.

"Who's the primary?"

Jeanette hesitates. "Gabriella Sinclair-Gault."

I can take it when they're lazy. I can take it when they babble.
Guess I've got to.

"It needs work," Jeanette cautions. "It's never been touched."

"Like that matters, Jeanette."

She laughs.

Every broker knows. Even if it had been touched, even if Gabriella convinces the sellers to let her stage it, the new people will
rip everything out. China White has to be Cameo White. Navajo
White, Moonstone. Raised panels? Recess them. If the hardware's
gold-plated, where's the polished nickel? Use somebody else's bathtub? Please. Rehabbing? No. Remodeling? Close. *Renovating!*
What we call "Making it your own."

"What line is the apartment, Jeanette?"

I can't hear her.

"What, Jeanette?"

"G," she whispers.

The Black Hole of Calcutta Line.

I dial Mrs. Sambaba at Sparkle.

"Mrs. Sambaba! Nanny Wunderlich here! What on earth
happened?"

"Oh my God in heaven! Mrs. Wunderlich, I tell you, my girls
come back, they cross themselves. Those toilets! And balls of white

hair everywhere! Every room! What they do? Voodoo? Must I be more explicit, Mrs. Wunderlich? And those drains! Both bathrooms!" She pronounces "both" "boat" and "bath" "bat." "I never send my girls where I would not go myself, Mrs. Wunderlich. I'm straight with you, yes? When elephants fight, it is the grass that suffers."

"Mrs. Sambaba. Forgive me. I should have warned you. You're talking about 1155 Park, right? The Hahns' apartment? I think there was a drug situation. The dentist and his wife are both in jail. Please tell your wonderful ladies I'm so sorry I forgot to mention the apartment was, um, unique. Please tell them that of course I'll double the usual fee. And I comprehend fully this job may take more hours than usual."

"Well I'm glad you understand." Mrs. Sambaba softens. "Of course, my girls will have to discard their mops. And buckets as well."

"Of course. New everything. Let me know how much."

"A professional is only as good as her equipment," Mrs. Sambaba says. "A saucy dog laps his own tail."

"I couldn't agree more, Mrs. Sambaba."

If you'd overheard this conversation, Freddy, you'd say, "Who's working for who?"

In the bedroom, I kick off my flats. All the women in our business wear them. They're part of the Upper East Side broker uniform. Comfortable enough to walk around in all day, but pricey enough to convince superficial people you're one of them. I get mine at the Memorial Sloan-Kettering Thrift Shop for fifteen dollars. Two hundred boxes of broker flats, remaindered like books. Bobbie was giddy: "You saved three hundred and forty-five dollars on those shoes," she said. "You owe yourself a three-hundred-and-forty-five-dollar present."

"I do?"

"And you can take the fifteen dollars off your taxes as a charitable donation to Memorial Hospital."

"I can?"

"The New Shopping Math," she called it. If you bought something on sale, you owed yourself the difference.

There was no one better to shop with. Or see a movie with. Or suss out a fresh listing. My pal. I have a hole in my heart as big as the Ritz.

The sun slides behind the monster high-rise that went up two years ago, lopping a vertical third off my view. Now I've got two-thirds trees and one-third OPW, Other People's Windows. In terms of real estate, I've slipped from "prk vu" to "partial prk vu." In the OPW across from mine, the man is flossing his teeth. He's wearing, what is that? A cummerbund? A truss?

I take a shower and cover myself in geranium lotion. I study my face in the mirror and try to remember what Flora said: Toner, then cleanser? Cleanser followed by toner? Rouge is "blush" now. Lipstick, "gloss." Aren't I too old for gloss? Is a fifty-nine-year-old supposed to look dewy? Perfume never sprayed on directly. Perfume sprayed in front of you, then, as the mist hangs in the air, speed through it.

I've had the bathroom to myself three years now, and it's still a surprise, toothpaste where I left it, no black whiskers punctuating the sink. Why is my stuff crowded on the bottom of the medicine chest? When will I sleep in the middle of the bed?

I cleanse. I spritz. Then the new thing, the Velvet Repair Mask. I open the box. Inside, six little ampoules huddle like baby birds in a nest. The Velvet Repair Mask comes with homework. Twelve pages of reading material. I can have a Velvet Repair Mask lesson in French, Italian, German, Spanish, Dutch, Portuguese, Swedish, Russian, a Middle Eastern language that looks like worms.

I snap an ampoule of Velvet Repair Mask, Hydratant Réparateur, Feuchtigkeit Spendende Aufbaumaske, Idratante Riparatore, Hidratante Reparadora, Hidratante Riparadora, Hydraterend Herstellend, and rub it in. It's okay. I dab some French perioral almond cream on my upper lip. Flora says it's six hundred dollars a bottle. For six hundred dollars it must be doing something. Then the Harvard doc's under-eye mousse, the Yale dermatologist's crow's-feet oil, the sexy Swiss widow's neck gel, the lip exfoliator that hurts a little but gets rid of dead lip, the lip crème that soothes the trauma from the lip exfoliator, the nasolabial-fold ointment that feels tingly, which means it must be working, applied in dabs with a dollhouse silver spoon, then spread across the face by taps with the ball of the fourth finger—the weakest hence least likely to maim. Flora has seen the enemy and it is rubbing.

A chamomile soufflé on heels and elbows induces softness and sleep. Lastly, spray pillow with lavender cologne. Even my pillow gets a treatment.

All this stash from Floradorable. If she loses her job, it's back to Lubriderm.

In the little room, I log on. The laptop trembles and sighs, like it's taking a deep breath before the work of connecting me to the universe. I check my e. There are four opportunities to get Viagra without a prescription, and two shots at refinancing a mortgage I don't have. I can consolidate my debt! Add inches where it really counts! Or lose five pounds this weekend! Spam, the finger on the pulse of American fear. How could Bobbie, of all people, have kept a secret? Why did she want Alice involved? Is this a two-woman job? Where's her card? I've got it here somewhere.

> From: nannypoo@aol.com
> To: Luba1102@earthlink.com
> Subject: the letter
> Dear Alice,
> Think we should get together to discuss Bobbie's letter? I do.
> Warmly, Nanny Wunderlich

To My Dearest Friends

I crawl into bed with Eli's egg salad and two raisin-walnut rolls. At last. There is something to be said for getting into a bed alone, something besides loneliness. I scissor my legs the full width. A scent, part fruit, part herb, wafts up.

I glance out the window. The man across the way is in his kitchen stirring a pot. The truss is gone. He's wearing a shower cap.

9 · Out of the Loop

Nanny Wunderlich lurches off the escalator on seven. She heads for the ladies' lounge. She is early. She has come to freshen up, not what her late husband referred to as "pump the bilge."

In the anteroom, she studies her reflection. She reapplies a viscous lip gloss called Kitty Mama. She fluffs her curly bangs by extending her lower lip and exhaling up. She thinks: I have a cast-iron bladder. I never have to go. This thought startles her. Has it come to this? she asks herself. Bladder pride?

Bergdorf's is building something new and they've annexed part of the lounge. It is smaller than it used to be and the marble walls are covered now with grass cloth. Despite this intrusion, Bergdorf's lounge remains her favorite ladies' room in New York. She plays a game she likes to play in small city spaces: What If I Have to Sell My Apartment and Live Here. She surveys the lounge and decides she could be happy by the window reading the paper every morning, sipping coffee, looking out at the park. Without the constant flushing, she could live here in a snap. She would leave the walls and marble floor just as they are and put in a Murphy bed. The east wall, solid bookcases with a narrow tufted fainting-couch. There was plenty of space and, in the business part, the plumbing for a shower and modest kitchen. The ladies' lounge in Bergdorf's was in move-in condition.

She takes the escalator to five. She soldiers through racks of Nanette Lepore suits and surfaces at Café on 5. Where she used to meet her friend for lunch, shoes are being sold. Café on 5 isn't there.

"Excuse me." She grabs the arm of a sales associate. "Am I on five? Where's Café on 5? Is this the fifth floor?"

"Café on 5 is Goodman's now," the woman says. "They moved it downstairs. In makeup."

"Café on 5 is in the basement?"

"It's Goodman's now."

Riding the down escalator, she releases a button on her jacket. It has long surrendered its original shape. She opens her handbag and fans herself with her checkbook.

In the basement, sales associates make themselves up, blinking against mascara wands, meshing lips. She winds through aisles of cosmetics and perfume. It feels like the girls' room on prom night. She spots an impromptu sign. Goodman's.

At the top of the steps, she takes in the new restaurant. It is smaller, plainer. The counter is gone. Goodman's looks like a mess hall. Happily, every table still sports a rose nosegay in a silver julep cup. Happily, the roses are still the color of thirties lingerie. It is good to see the brownies by the cash register stacked precisely as the pyramids. It is good to see Michael, the old maître d'.

Waiters wait, alert by the kitchen door. Expectation fills the air. It is 11 a.m., a weekday midmorning. Goodman's is poised for lunch.

"What's the story, Michael?" she says. "How come you moved down here?"

"Guess how many salads you have to sell to equal one pair of Kors stilettos, sweetie."

"That okay?" She points to the banquette in a far corner. From that vantage point, she will be able to see the action. She will be able to watch the stream of life, Bergdorf-style. Timeless women with streaked manes and upholstered headbands who dress the way their mothers dressed for lunch at Bergdorf's one generation ago. New Jersey strutters in slacks and fur jackets who hold their heads high. Elderly mothers whose patient, aging daughters politely pull their chairs. New mothers pushing new daughters in strollers. Old friends haggling over the check. Women who lunch alone wearing hats. They chew gazing into the middle distance.

"How many are you, dear?" Michael asks.

"Two."

He leads Nanny to the banquette and deposits two menus. She checks. Yes, what she wants is still there. She glances toward the entrance of the café. She supposes Alice Vogel will make the same mistake she did and go to five. She hopes the waitress won't wait to bring the bread.

Alice appears at the cash register. Spotting Nanny, she strides to the table.

"I do hope I'm not late."

"You're in the ballpark."

"I went to five," Alice explains.

"Same here. So welcome to the Gulag, Alice. I mean, this isn't even the basement. It's the sub-basement."

An out-of-work actress with spiky orange hair appears.

"Can I get you ladies some Perrier?"

"Tap water will be fine," Alice says. "And I'd like a Gotham. If you still make them."

The waitress bobs her head. She is asked this a hundred times a day.

"Me too." Nanny turns to Alice. "Bobbie loved the Gotham."

"Yes," Alice says. "I know."

The women look at each other. Their friend has been dead three weeks. Thoughts of her are accompanied by a fresh need to absorb that, a bucket of water over the head every time.

"I hate when they push the Perrier," Nanny breaks the silence.

A Bergdorf's model sweeps by their table. Her head rocks side to side, as if her neck is stirring it.

"That'll be in Luba next year for five hundred dollars."

"They eat cotton balls to fill their stomachs," Nanny says. "And check the fingernails. I don't get it. What is it about high-maintenance women? Give a guy a choice between a high-maintenance chick and a natural beauty, he'll take high-maintenance every time."

"Men prefer a woman who looks like she's gone to lengths to attract him. That she's invested hours to catch his eye. Think of natural selection," Alice says.

"But they're counter-natural. They're caricatures. I'd never want a high-maintenance man. Would you?"

"I appreciate a man who takes care of himself."

"Colorless nail polish on a guy?" Nanny says. "Ew. The Senate in session looks like a hairdressers' convention. Why does every Hollywood producer have hair that looks like he's stuck his finger in a socket?"

"You wanted to have lunch?"

"We need to discuss next steps."

"Next steps?" Alice says.

"The letter. Were you surprised?"

"Actually," Alice replies, "I had no idea."

"Me neither."

"Statistically," Alice continues, "most marriages aren't faithful. So although Roberta failed to mention it, in that sense, no, I am not the least bit surprised. Nor, may I add, do I care."

The waitress ferries two glasses of ice water and a bread basket. Nanny peers in. She removes a fetal piece of whole wheat. "You know," she adds, "I always thought Jack and Bobbie were happy."

"They were," Alice says. "A romp does not preclude that. They married terribly young. That's how Jack avoided Vietnam."

"Did you march?"

"Everybody did."

Nanny opens the gold foil on a butter pat. The restaurant fills. In ten minutes, there will be a line.

‌‍‌‌‌‌

"Well," Nanny says, "I guess a lot of people have secrets. Even Bobbie."

"Of course," Alice says. "That's what separates us from the apes. Everyone has secrets. Don't you?"

Nanny pauses. She takes inventory. Raising her chin, she says, "I've done nothing to be ashamed of."

"Alas." Alice steals a look at her watch. "Look. I don't think Roberta would appreciate us dishing about her, do you?"

"We're not dishing. You call this dishing? Here's what I think. She didn't leave instructions. So we've got to talk about her. How else can we figure it out? Don't think of it as dish. Think of it as an assignment from a dead friend."

"Assignment? All right then. Why do you think Roberta wanted us to see the letter?"

"Let's start with: Maybe she didn't."

"Then why have us sign the vault card?" Alice says.

"Maybe she thought she'd have time to go back to the vault, but just in case, you and me, we're Plan B."

"Were that the case, Roberta would have told us flat-out."

"So where are we?" Nanny asks.

"Completely in the dark," Alice says, "at Bergdorf's. Look, dear. It's reckless speculation thinking we can divine what Roberta wanted. What she wanted is unknowable. If she had wanted us to take action, surely she would have been explicit."

"You're saying Bobbie left us the letter to reveal the secret but not have us do anything about it?"

"All we know for certain is, Roberta may have wanted us to have the information. I say 'may' because perhaps you're right and she couldn't get back to the vault before she died. Perhaps she wanted us to destroy the letter for her. In either case, I vote for no further action. Frankly, I'd rather do nothing than the wrong thing."

The Gothams arrive, alps of confettied salad. It was their friend's favorite. Every morsel chopped the same size, no ungainly ruffled-lettuce sheaf to hack, or skidding tomato wedges to chase around the plate. The Gotham was diced, no work, and every bite tasted of many things—Gruyère, bacon, ham, turkey, tomatoes, greens, all tossed with a pale pink dressing.

Alice wonders how she can finish it.

Nanny takes her first bite and sees a hole where salad used to be.

"Good grief!" Alice says. "This is so much food. This is why America is fat."

"The Gotham at Bergdorf's?" Nanny says. "You know what I'm thinking, Alice? I'm thinking it's kind of elaborate, paying for a box to hide one measly letter."

"And where would you hide 'one measly letter' that had the potential to destroy your marriage and devastate your child?"

"In a book they'd never read."

"And what might that be?"

Nanny thinks. *"Tattooing for Dummies."*

"A perfect diversion," Alice says.

"Edith Hamilton's *Mythology.*"

"A basic reference."

"Something really fat, doorstop-fat, like *Moby-Dick.*"

"I'm reading that right now."

"In the freezer." Nanny is exasperated. "In Tupperware marked GIZZARDS."

"It is possible," Alice says, "Roberta didn't know what to do with it."

"If a man wrote me a letter like that, I sure as hell couldn't destroy it," Nanny says.

"Yes. But would you want other people to read it?"

"Maybe it's just Bobbie telling us one last secret."

"Ironic." Alice's voice softens. "Roberta believed telling secrets was good for your health."

Nanny nods. "The Pennebaker theory. Self-disclosure boosts the immune system. It reduces shame and guilt."

"Is that common knowledge?"

"In the field. Dr. Pennebaker wrote *Opening Up*. You know, Alice, a lot of secrets Bobbie told, she didn't use names."

It occurs to Alice that Roberta may have told Nanny about Mr. Wald.

"That does not make one shred of difference." Alice keeps her voice even. "A confidence is a confidence. Whether or not it is attributed. A secret is not something to dine out on."

"Okay, Alice. Okay. Just let me get this straight: You think we should chuck the letter, forget we saw it?"

"Precisely."

"Then why didn't Bobbie toss it?"

"Consider the element of exhibitionism: *Look how much I was loved.* Or perhaps it was: *Look how much fun I had.* Perhaps she believed she'd be cured, hence keep it in the box and visit it. In which case, we would not be having lunch. We never would have seen it."

"That can't be it," Nanny says. "Nope."

"And why not?"

"She wouldn't have had us sign the card."

"But if Roberta knew she was dying and we hadn't signed, Jack and Betsy, as her heirs, would have opened the box."

"Alice. If she kept the letter for us, there has to be a reason. It wasn't an accident. It was planned. The net-net is, I agree we can't know for sure what she wanted. That said, I've got a theory."

Nanny waits for a response. When none comes, she proceeds. "In his letter he wrote something about *her* letter. Bobbie wanted her lover to have his letter back."

"Well she hardly needed two friends for that. She could have mailed it to him."

Nanny finishes her salad and reaches for more bread.

"What do you think, Alice? Think Jack knew?"

"What an idea!" Alice coughs.

"You all right?" Nanny asks.

"Aspirated . . . ham . . ."

"Don't talk." Nanny pushes Alice's water glass closer. "Raise your left arm."

Alice raises her arm. The cough subsides. She takes a sip of water, concentrating as it works its way down. When she trusts her recovery, Alice says, "Thank you."

"He didn't put the year on the letter," Nanny persists. "This could have happened five years ago. Ten."

"How is that relevant?"

"The letter's dated Thursday, August first," Nanny says.

"What difference does it make when it was written?"

"I don't know. Maybe it would tell us something. Don't you think it's weird there's a letter, period? I mean, who writes letters anymore?"

"Lovers will always write letters," Alice says. "After the invention of the phone, Yeats wrote Maude Gonne every day." She pats her lips with her napkin. "Here's what I think. I think you're much more invested in this than I am. I run a business. My mother is far from well. My eldest is expecting his first child in five weeks. Having an affair is hardly the Second Coming. Whatever Roberta's plan was, she took it to the grave."

"Um."

"Anything we try to think of is . . . Look, I'm loath to say it again, but it's reckless speculation."

"The old rec spec."

The waitress whisks up Nanny's plate.

"Still working on that?" she says to Alice.

Alice shakes her head. The waitress removes her plate as well.

"I hate that," Nanny says. "Since when is eating a job?"

"You know," Alice says, "Roberta liked to play with people."

"Huh?"

"I am not implying she was malevolent. I wouldn't say that. But she courted mischief. That said"—Alice leans in—"I could see her writing this letter merely to drive us mad."

"Excuse me?" Nanny shakes her head. "Are we talking about the same person?"

"I so wish Roberta had kept this to herself. Did you ever have information you wish you didn't have?"

"Have you?"

"Who hasn't?"

"Well," Nanny says, "you're talking to a lapsed therapist. I think all info is good."

"Do you." Alice purses her lips.

"Isn't it always better to know?"

"No."

"Why not?" Nanny says.

"Because you can't *un*know something."

"It's not about having the information," Nanny says. "It's what you do with it."

The model slinks to their table. She strikes a pose. Gold hoops with a five-inch diameter pierce her ears. Her black dress twists like a Möbius strip.

"This is Issey Miyake. You will find it on three. It is available for two thousand nine hundred eighty-five dollars."

She pirouettes to another table.

"Jeez," Nanny says, "that's more than my first car."

Alice signals the waitress. She takes out her American Express card. "I've got to get going. We can split this right down the middle. We both had Gothams."

Nanny pokes through her bag. "Where's my card?"

"If you give me cash, I'll put it on mine."

"*Quanto?*"

"Thirty-two forty and, let's see, a six-dollar tip?"

"Ten," Nanny says. "She's a struggling actress."

"Fine."

Nanny frisks her pockets. She pushes a pile of crumpled bills toward Alice.

"I owe you twenty cents," she says.

Alice flattens the bills and sorts them by denomination. "And what is your next step, may I ask?"

" '*Your*'? You're not in this with me?"

"Clearly you're taking this quite seriously," Alice says. "And I'm so glad we had this lunch. But I'm afraid I'm out of the loop."

"Are you suggesting, and I think you are, that we do nothing with the letter?"

"Not at all. No. Please feel free to do whatever you care to with the letter. That said, I do think you'd be wise to leave it alone. You have no idea where this might take you. The potential for hurting Jack and Betsy is incalculable. Beyond that, my sense of it is, there's no indication Roberta wanted us to do anything. It's a fool's errand."

"A friend's errand. Don't you feel you owe Bobbie something?"

"How can the living owe the dead? I was the best friend I could be to Roberta when she was alive."

"But Alice. You have to admit. We have a responsibility to her."

"No. I don't. I don't have to admit anything. A posthumous obligation? I'm afraid I don't see it that way."

Harshness creeps into Nanny's voice: "She did this for a reason. Us ignoring it can't be her intention."

"You know," Alice says with care, "it's possible Roberta wasn't in her right mind before she died. That it metastasized to her brain."

Nanny narrows her eyes. "I saw her the day before, Alice. So screw that, okay? Bobbie was on the ball to the end."

Alice pushes her chair back. Nanny understands. Alice is offended. This is her dismiss signal.

"You won't help?" Nanny tries one last time.

Alice rises. "I wish I could."

Nanny whoops. Heads turn. Alice starts to smile. *I wish I could.* Both women remember their friend saying, *I wish I could.* It was the phrase she used instead of *No. I wish I could* was how she got out of doing anything she didn't want to without vexing the person she was turning down.

They stop laughing, then start up again.

"All right." Alice sits down. "I'm fairly certain I can pinpoint which particular Thursday, August first, the letter was written, what year, although I don't see how it would help."

"How could you do that?"

"My date books. I've kept them since college. Roberta and I ran every morning. The letter was dated August first. He said he would see her a day or two from when she received it. That would make it around August fifth. If she was out of town, or she couldn't run with me, I'd have jotted that down."

"That's great, Alice. How far back can you check?"

"Thirty-nine years."

"She's stupid," Mother remarks. She pronounces it with three syllables, "stee-you-pid."

I fluff her pillows. When she dies, no one will hear "stee-you-pid" again.

"Mother, I want you to try your very best to like Murlene."

"She has a gangrenous heart."

"No, *Maman chérie*. She's kind. She wants to please."

"Oh, what do you know, Alice? *Tu n'es jamais ici.*"

This is only semi-true. Twice a week, for one hour, I am here.

"Sadists are drawn to nursing," Mother continues. "Just as bullies are drawn to police work and pedophiles to the priesthood."

I slide a Horchow catalog under Mother's water glass. Its wet bottom has left a white welt on the Empire end table that will one day be mine. "Oh really Mother. Frankie. Violet. Lily. Now Murlene."

"You mustn't discredit me because I'm old. Don't do it, Alice. You won't like it when you're my age and Jason and David patronize you."

"I have sons, Mother. I'll be in assisted living."

"I warned you to keep going till you got a girl."

"I'm going to take that as a compliment, *Maman*."

I rip off a spoon stuck to *Vogue*. Perhaps Murlene is an ax-murderer. Perhaps she beats Mother on the soles of her feet with a rubber hose. Who knows what Murlene does when I am not visiting. Anyone can be a saint two hours a week.

"I brought your favorite sandwich, *Maman*." I open a brown bag. "And a chocolate egg cream."

"Don't spill that egg cream," she warns. "Chocolate is quite impossible to get out."

The "quite" makes me smile. My mother, first-generation American, with Russian and French parents who spoke Yiddish at home. *Quite. Vulgar. Uncouth. Stee-you-pid.* And my favorite, *crass.*

"Yes, I know all about the hazards of chocolate, Mother."

"Now don't take that tone with me, miss. You were perfectly happy with vanilla until your classmates at Brearley exposed you to chocolate."

Oh those wicked chocolate-scarfing ruffians.

I slice the sandwich into quarters.

"Where's yours?" Mother asks.

"I brought one for you and one for Murlene. I've got *Zauberflöte* with Charles tonight."

"Why on earth did you bring Murlene one? You're going to spoil her."

"Here, Mother. Look how fresh the rye is."

She lifts a corner of the bread as if inspecting a mousetrap. "There's no Russian!"

I pass Mother a small plastic cup. "You like it on the side."

"Schrafft's had the best Russian. Nothing comes close. What happened to Schrafft's, Alice? How could it go under? I tell you, I will absolutely never understand."

Everyone who ate there is dead. Except you, *Maman.*

"It was the only place in town you could get a hot-fudge sundae with your martini. Ask Murlene to bring a little plate, would you, dear? This is too much for me. I could never eat all this. What time is it?"

"Five-fifteen."

"What? Why am I eating dinner at five-fifteen? What kind of name is 'Murlene'?" Mother shakes her head. "I like strong names. You chose good names for the boys, Alice."

Oh Mother. You chose the names. Don't you remember? I believed you knew best. Even what to call my sons.

She settles into her sandwich.

Since the progression of Mother's spinal stenosis, she has confined herself to bed. Except for events like appointments with doctors and Roberta's funeral, Mother refuses to be seen in a wheelchair. She wants to be remembered the way she was, glorious in Grès, sailing tall up Madison Avenue, the prow of New York. Charlotte Fargotstein Kaye, flawless proprietress of Luba, doyenne of provenanced couture. A woman designed for clothes.

The hospital tray clears Mother's flaccid thighs. A starched white napkin drapes it. She guzzles the egg cream.

"Emily Post says you're entitled to two slurps." Mother drains the waxed cup.

"She does not."

"Are you contradicting me?"

A shard of turkey lands on the carpet. Picking it up, I come across a desiccated apple core and the hoary side of a toothed Oreo. I wipe a chewed bit of rye off Mother's chin. What happens to people that they no longer feel food on their chins?

"Now, darling. Tell me. Didn't you have an appointment with Roberta's attorney last week?"

"I did."

"What on earth was that about?"

Do I tell my mother Roberta had a lover? Ask her advice? Secrets compound. Now Roberta's secret is my secret as well.

"That darling girl," Mother continues. "You were a perfect friend to her. Just as I was to her mother. What did the lawyer want? Did it have anything to do with the commune?"

"The Berkshire Plan?"

"Your Aunt Edith and I were going to have such a marvelous old age looking in on each other. Hiring a cook. A driver too. Pooling our resources. What was your name for it, dear?"

"Innisfree."

"We were hoping you girls would carry it on. Now your Aunt Edith is dead. And darling Roberta, dead as a doornail too."

And what would have happened to you in the Berkshires, Mother? Aunt Edith smoothing your sheepskin sheet? You nursing Aunt Edith from a wheelchair?

A waste of breath the years behind
In balance with this life, this death

There's nothing one can go through Yeats hasn't first. W.B. paves the way.

Mother continues. "We've both lost our best friends, Alice. Are you wearing the bracelet?"

"Of course."

"Give me your arm. I want to see."

She clutches my wrist in papery hands.

"That girl." Mother shakes her head. "She made me laugh. What a loss."

Are you having fun up there, Roberta? Throwing me together with your friend? And that's not the end of it. Watch. I'll have to have lunch with her again.

"Mother. I've never asked you. Do you have secrets?"

"I'm human, Alice. What would you like to know?"

"Nothing in particular. I was just wondering."

"Here. Would you like a secret? I'll tell you Aunt Sylvie's secret. Would you like that, dear?"

"Yes."

"Aunt Sylvie wore an inflatable brassiere. She blew it up with a weensy straw every morning before breakfast."

"Mother. That's hilarious!"

"The point is, Alice dear. Everybody's secrets are ridiculous except to the person whose secret it is. Now tell me," she continues. "What's happening at Luba?"

"Mrs. Vandervoort was in."

"Anything good?"

"Two Oscars and a Carolina."

"Did she buy anything?"

"No."

"What you want, Alice, is Mrs. Vandervoort's granddaughter. You want the next generation. John Galliano, Proenza Schouler, Hussein Chalayan, that's your future. Did you straighten things out with the accountant?"

"I have to call him."

"Watch out for Fleischman, darling. He used to chase me in the back. The man has itchy fingers."

"Mother!"

"But he's a good friend to Luba. Listen to him, Alice. I mean it."

"Mr. Fleischman can't make clients come in, Mother."

"You should be bustling now, Alice. It's fall. Fall is a marvelous time for Luba."

"Nobody is shopping, Mother. *Personne.*"

"You're not going to bring cheap things in, promise me, Alice. Don't let the notion of volume fool you. The more high-end the merchandise, the more selective you are, the more you net. Luba must maintain its distinction from other consignment shops."

"So you've mentioned, *Maman.*"

"Luba must be thought of as a place to find *la chose exquise,* Alice. Not Bargaintown. As soon as you let anything cheap in, you're like everybody else."

"Yes, Mother."

"Now tell me. I can't wait to hear. What is Luba wearing today? How does she look?"

"I was thinking of letting Yumi change her."

"The intern? Really, you give the help much too much leeway. I never trusted anyone else to dress Luba. If a woman passes Luba on the Number 2 bus, she must leap off at the next stop. The window has to be that seductive, *chérie.*"

"*D'accord, Maman.*"

"If things are slow, you might consider changing the split. It needn't be fifty-fifty. It could be sixty-forty."

"That would never work."

"You're contradicting me again?"

"Mother, why would people consign with Luba if they could get more money elsewhere?"

"That's always been your problem, Alice. A *crise de confidence.* Now tell me. Where is Charles taking you Christmas?"

"We haven't decided. It depends on Jason and the baby."

She stares at me. "I don't like the way you look, Alice. Are you being nice to Charles?"

What does she mean?

"You haven't told him anything you might not be able to take back, have you?"

"Mother!" What does she know?

"Why don't you go to Sicily?"

Because my husband is in private practice, Mother. Because my husband works without a net. Because not every New York lawyer can charge five hundred dollars an hour.

"Your father and I had a glorious time at Huntington Hartford's place in Nassau."

Certainly, Mother. The moment we win the lottery.

"Darling, do you remember that trip?"

"Everybody stared at you in the dining room, Mother."

"No one believed I could be the mother of a teen-ager! I'm glad you know how to take care of yourself, Alice."

"I had the best teacher."

"You could still turn a few heads if you'd wear a bit of eye-liner."

"I have on lip gloss, Mother. See?"

"Well it's too light. Women over fifty can't wear pink."

Red handbag, red shoes. No piqué before Memorial Day. Princess-length pearls at lunch. Opera-length at night. Unless you're over forty. Rules. But yes, Mother. I know. I can still turn heads.

"I was thinking of getting you a little computer, Mother. Is that something you might like? You could type on your tray."

"Now what would I do with a computer, Alice? If you'd like to immolate some money, set a match to it."

"You could e-mail Jason and David every day. Your great-grandchildren will be growing up with it."

"I have no use for such a thing."

"They come with built-in encyclopedias."

"I have the 1958 Britannica. Cost your papa a pretty penny. And I never use that one."

"You can find out about anybody in the world."

"You mean snoop?"

"You can get the *Times*."

"Why would I want to read a big newspaper on a little machine?"

"You can shop. All the stores are on line."

"Darling, please. I get every catalog there is. From Abercrombie's to Zuni handicrafts."

"But Mother, if you can go to the doctor in your wheelchair, if you can go to Roberta's funeral, why can't you meet me at Bergdorf's for lunch?"

"You want me to go where I once held court *in a wheelchair*?"

I push her tray aside. I move to the edge of her bed.

"Alice!"

"*Maman.*"

"What are you doing!"

I circle my arms around her shoulders.

"Alice! Stop that!" She thrashes like a washing machine. "This instant!"

I kiss her widening part. She smells like Pond's cold cream and arnica.

"Alice, are you out of your mind?"

Her birdy elbows push through the angora bed jacket.

I let her go.

She smooths her hair. "If you love me so much, get rid of that witch."

"What does Murlene do, exactly, that displeases you so?"

"Watch." Mother picks up a crystal bell. When I was growing up, that bell rested on the dining-room table to the right of her spoon.

Mother rings. She raises her chin and cocks an ear. No "Coming!" emanates from the depths of the apartment. No rapid tap of footsteps charges the air.

"See?" Mother hisses.

"I'm taking this." I slip the bell into my handbag. "You cannot ring for a human anymore. Those days are gone, Mother. People don't like to be rung for. Murlene is not chattel."

She crosses her arms over her chest. "Then find me chattel, Alice. I want chattel."

"Mur-lene?" I trill. In a moment she is there.

"Yes?" Murlene says, pleasant enough.

"Murlene dear," Mother takes over, "would you be so kind as to put up some tea for us? And a few of those shortbread cookies? If any are left."

"Do you want English Breakfast or the Ceylon, Mrs. Kaye?"

"The English Breakfast in the red tin. Don't use too much. And rinse the pot with boiling water before you fill it. And only let the tea steep four minutes."

"Same as always, Mrs. Kaye."

When Murlene leaves the room, Mother says: "What I really miss are the girls."

Mother's best friends: Aunt Sylvie, Aunt Dorothy, Aunt Belle, and Roberta's mother, Aunt Edith. She has outlived them all. I have only outlived Roberta.

"Mother. You can play bridge on the computer."

"Bridge?"

"Yes. And canasta."

While I tell her how pretty the computers are and how she can take lessons, Murlene comes in with a tray.

"Put that here." Mother points a perfectly manicured finger.

Hands flying, she readies the tea. If only I knew more tasks that summon this overdrive. I drift around the room, touching her things, the involuntary inventory. I do not wish to take it but have given up trying not to: The bureau scarred by medicine bottles left by nurses who knew they were not coming back. It will have to be refinished. The lovely récamier with fatal stains. It will have to be re-covered. The bedroom set the boys can fight over if their wives have any interest. The boulle jewelry box with the crystal intaglio that was off-limits when I was a child. The matching Meissen butterfly bed-lamps. Butterflies. Could I still turn heads?

I gather last week's dead flowers and make a note to send up tulips. Mother's bedroom window is on the park. I pull her drapes. The trees look like sketches. Surely the grisaille of late fall in New York will cheer her. I want my mother to still want to see the change of seasons.

I collect and straighten magazines. When my circle is complete, I sit next to Mother for a parting cup. Our visit is drawing to a close. Tea, the home stretch.

"Tell me about the commune, Mother."

"You've heard all this before, Alice. A million times. Is that why Roberta's lawyer wanted to see you?"

"You're so smart, Mother."

"We were going to get land near Tanglewood. Build lovely little houses with lovely little porches. Have a communal kitchen. Your Aunt Edith knew another couple who wanted to as well. She thought I'd like them. Everybody would have privacy but everybody would be nearby. We wouldn't trouble our children. We'd look in on each other. If you were missing at a meal, someone would knock on your door." She takes a sip. "And if need be"— Mother puts down her cup—"there would be someone who cared enough to wipe food off your chin."

11 · Fundamental Magic Words

Why did Alice ask me if I had any secrets? Who doesn't have secrets?

"Did you see that layup, Mom?" Flora shouts.

What's it Alice's business I had to take my boards twice. Who needs to know Freddy used a rose to beat the draft, or how many abortions I had.

"You're not watching, Mom!"

Bobbie meant to go back and get the letter. Bet that's it. The vault was her hiding place. But then why leave both of us the key? She knew she was dying. No doubt about that. What do you hide when you know you're going to die? What do you destroy?

The announcer screams something about a full-court press. It can't have anything to do with ironing. Will this game ever end? Will I ever see my bed again?

Our seats are center-court. Flora's magazine is being wooed by the publicist of a Brazilian bikini-waxer. I suppose it's not surprising Brazil has maintained its edge as world leader of bikini waxing. Maybe, in the end, Alice is right. So Bobbie had a lover. So what. Like Alice said: most marriages, there's a lover. Ones like mine, they're the oddballs.

Finally the Knicks prevail. A grown man from the blue team hunches under the basket and weeps into his shirt. Madison Square Garden empties with exuberant exhaustion. The air feels secondhand, like it's been in a balloon. I inch behind Flora toward the nearest exit sign. The smell is beer-soaked concrete and stale popcorn. We shuffle out of New York's ugliest building and I get to watch men ogle my daughter. Flora wears her beauty like a bagel-coat, something you throw over your pajamas to pick up Nova Sunday morning. That other people stare confirms it's not just mother-love that makes my daughter worth noting. I'm grateful she's unaware of her effect, but it scares me too. It's dangerous not to know you're beautiful. Flora, five foot ten, scrubbed, with black hair so lustrous you could read by it. What's that thing sticking out of her bun? Is that a chopstick? Amazing, two normaloids producing a Flora.

Outside, a vendor hawks roasted chestnuts. What other food makes you think of a song?

"Let's walk to Sixth," Flora says. "We'll have a better chance at a cab."

She grabs my hand like she did when she was two. I love getting my hand grabbed. The other worst part of Freddy's death was Flora's mint vulnerability. No grandparents, no father, no sibs. She worries about me. I worry about her. You get through terrible things trying to make them better for other people.

On Sixth Avenue, she stands in the street. Facing traffic, Flora raises her arm. She used to be the one on the sidewalk. A cab screeches over. She holds the door for me and leans in to give the driver instructions. We fasten our seat belts. With any luck, I'll be in bed in twenty minutes.

"Mom," Flora says, "which one of us you think'll get married first?"

"I hope you're not waiting for me, puss."

"I want you to be happy, Mommy. And please don't say, 'I'm happy if you're happy.' "

"But it's true."

"It's tyranny."

"Okay, let's change the subject. How's Betsy?"

"I don't know."

"You didn't call her for tonight?"

"Aunt Bobbie just died, Ma."

"It's been three weeks, sweetheart. Betsy could use some distraction."

"You're always pushing us together, Mom."

"You love Betsy!"

"Everything she does is so perfect. How come you never criticize her?"

"I don't have to. She's not my daughter."

"You wish I was in the arts. You wish I was a composer too."

"Right. Like I want my daughter to take a vow of poverty."

"Okay. My turn to change the subject. Are you dating yet, Mom?"

"Nope."

"I'm doing the Hunt but you can't tell anyone."

"Who would I tell? And besides, everything you tell me is secret unless you say otherwise."

"Like you didn't tell Aunt Bobbie stuff about me?"

"Only when I needed advice. Never when I thought it might hurt you. Your Aunt Bobbie gave wonderful advice. So tell me, why is doing the Hunt a secret? Internet dating is a sane way to meet people, no?"

Do I tell her? I've tried the Hunt. My evenings are conspicuously free. Not that I feel a hint of desperation. I've done marriage, had that experience. And the men in my age group look like my grandfather. Geezers surfing the Web for a "Saks-style woman," whatever that is. Or a Heidi yearning to yodel with them on the Appalachian Trail. Sixty-year-old men who actually write, "I'm not going to beat around the bush. Ha-ha," lusting for "big boobs and long legs." Really? You mean you don't want long boobs and big legs? Julian Barnes is in my age group. How come no men on the Hunt look like Julian Barnes? I will not date a man who thinks acid reflux is a conversational gambit. Or kiss a man with a white coating on his tongue. What is that white coating? Where are the sixty-something men who'd make out in a car? Have picnics in bed? I could never love a man in whom all boy was lost. Do you have to know a man when he was a boy to still see boy in him? When you looked at me, Freddy, did you still see girl? I'll never know a man again who knew me when I was young. Even you, Freddy, with your gastrointestinal hi-fidelity and flocculated comb-over, even with all your Freddy-as-hero stories, you had boy in you yet. There was bounce in your Wallabys. You got excited about the geopolitical ramifications of the Three Gorges Dam. You dared eat a hot dog.

"Ma." Flora kisses the air in my direction. "I want you to fall in love. I mean, don't you miss married life?"

Married life? What does that mean? Is she asking about sex? Companionship? A man willing to pick up Tampax on his way home? I could never love someone the way I loved Freddy. We can't have a history. We won't be able to dream of a lifetime together. Okay, maybe I would like one more shot at being loved right. Is it a terrible thing to think you might know the last time in your life you ever made love? What if we hadn't that morning? What if I hadn't put butter on his pancakes? What if we hadn't gone for a run? I miss loving a man. But if I was with a man now, even though I couldn't have imagined it when Fred was alive, I'd miss being alone. Being alone, sometimes it's heady. "Flora, I don't feel any pressure to meet somebody. I've had a husband."

"Don't you want to get married again, Ma?"

"There are things at my age that get exciting because there is no man."

"Like?"

And everything I think of saying seems stupid: Like knowing what's in the fridge is where you left it. Like never having to check with someone before you do something. Not making the bed. Little selfish things. Selfish is seductive after decades of putting yourself last. Of course I'd rather have you, Freddy. But I can't. So now sometimes I think what I'd really like is an affectionate studpuppy three or four nights a week who'd tuck me in and slip back to his own place. Life is an unknown now, in a way it wasn't before. How can I explain this welcome surprise to Flora? How do I praise being alone to my fatherless daughter? What I can do is show Flora that if your life doesn't go according to plan, you can be all right. I can—example? demonstrate? *model*—I can model resiliency. If the most important thing in the world is not to hurt your child, all of life after the birth of that child is a reckoning of how little you can actually do to protect it. Here you are, stuck with the fiercest thing you feel, and a dauntingly limited way to ensure its passage. "What I miss most, darling," I say, "is being Number One to somebody." Who cares when I leave town? Who calls when it's the first snowfall to say, "Look out the window"? Who wonders what I think about a hairy new fruit from Madagascar or says the fundamental magic words, "How was your day?"

"You're Number One to me, Mommy." Flora is earnest.

"That is an extremely temporary situation," I say. "Please God."

The moon is bold. We open our windows. Leaves ferment. The air smells like a Macoun. Two days before Thanksgiving, fall's swan song. Time to dig out the boots. How do people live without the change of seasons? Why do I need a man when I can speed up Broadway sucking crystalline New York air next to my daughter?

I drop her off at Ninety-sixth and Broadway and cut through the park. How brilliant Olmsted and Vaux were to blast the transverses below eye level. How fine it is to sail through Central Park in a timeless cavern of Manhattan schist. Headlights bounce off the mica. It's a regular twinkle-fest. I'm riding in a valley of stars.

12 · Die Zauberflöte

From: Luba1102@earthlink.com
To: nannypoo@aol.com
Subject: letter
Nanny—The only Thursday, August 1, since 1985
was 1991, 1996, and 2002. In 2002, Roberta and I
did not run the 4th, 5th, and 6th. My date books
prior to 1985 are down in the bin. Hope this helps.
Alice Vogel
Proprietress, Luba
1102 Madison Avenue
New York, New York 10028

Roberta adored the crossword too. Every time we came back to it, we would see connections we had not noticed before. We would read the clue a new way and suddenly what stymied was obvious. She did Sunday in a flash. Despite, on occasion, filling it incorrectly. The clue was an eight-letter word for KITSCH. Roberta wrote in KINCAIDE. She made the entire puzzle work around KINCAIDE even though the correct answer was BADTASTE. Puzzle clues are metaphors, the quickest way to say something without saying it. Like poetry. That ancient tribe in Siberia that plans for the future speaking only in metaphor. When asked why, they say, "Because the gods don't understand metaphor. They can't thwart us if they don't understand us."

Let's see. Six across. Five-letter word for BEST. PRIZE? No. Nine down can't start with Z.

What could be more pleasurable than doing the puzzle, sipping

Pinot Grigio in a lovely restaurant, with *Die Zauberflöte* for dessert? Tamino will get his Pamina. Papageno his Papagena. Should I tell Charles about Roberta's letter? Would he observe his own failing in it? It is hardly his fault. You're pulpy now, my darling, like an orphaned cucumber marooned behind the Tropicana. It's a miracle I don't have repetitive stress syndrome. My wrist, my fingers, a human camshaft sliding into prickled numbness. How does my hand on you compare with your hand on you? Dearest darling Charles. Within the first month of marriage, I learned. Your idea of pleasing me was making me come. You were so proud.

PROUD? No. Could BEST be OUTDO?

And what did I know? I became very good at coming, a comer *par excellence. Veni, veni, veni.* What pleasure did you get from me, Charles? When you rolled off and gasped, "Do me by hand"?

I might show him the letter. It would be interesting to get his take. On the other hand, he didn't care for Roberta:

"She's got something to say about everything."

"True. She has opinions."

Charles is unused to female opinion. I can listen as if the rest of the world has fallen away. I am an endangered species, a New York geisha. So few people listen well anymore, it has become exotic.

What kind of mood will Charles be in tonight? The clues are there, as familiar as a four-letter word for NEEDLECASE or three-letter word for CRUMB. Charles is my ETUI, my ORT. No. I won't mention the letter. The measure of a person is the secrets they keep.

PLUMS? Could BEST be PLUMS?

Mr. Wald will be my secret forever. And anyone else, should I be so blessed. Will I have another Mr. Wald? Dear Mr. Wald. The lecture was on insects. Jason had collected forty-two specimens and was cataloging them. It was wonderful charting Jason's growth spurred by collecting. Collections taught memory skills, visual acuity, patience. Jason liked all of it, stalking, classification, mounting. He enjoyed making the boxes. A ten-year-old wielding an X-Acto knife.

At camp his collection expanded. And then what happened? Was it puberty? When I e-mail Jason now, I include bug news. How the Asian long-horned beetle is attacking the park. If the strange bug on the kitchen window might be *Leptoglossus occidentalis.* Jason fails to respond in kind. Might it be, perhaps, time to let go?

How that boy pored over his bugs on his little oak desk. I'd sit next to him with my nose in his hair. The grime under his fingernails before I gave him a tub, the dimples at the base of his fingers, the sensual aspect of mothering and devastating withdrawal from it, as large a transition in a life as puberty or senility. The deprivation was profound. A way of loving up in smoke. You could wean a baby off a breast. But how do you wean a mother off the claim to sustain? You go from holding them and washing them and feeding them and dressing them and rocking them their every waking moment. And each day they need these things less and less until the day comes when the most you can get is the generic hug they give their peers.

PRIME?

David collected too. Baseball cards. He memorized statistics. He was the one who liked to eat, who dropped his toys and ran when he heard the suck of the refrigerator door. By two, he hadn't said "Mama" yet. How I worked with that boy! "Watch my mouth, David. 'Ma-Ma-Ma-Ma.' Watch my mouth." Sitting him on the kitchen counter, "Ma-Ma-Ma," his eyes glued to my lips. And then one day he tucked them in. "Mmmmmm." *Here it comes,* I thought. *Here it comes, David's first word!* "Mmmmmmm." It's coming! It's coming! And he said, "Mmm . . . ma . . . mayonnaise."

These touchable boys, married to California girls. I never should have let them go to Stanford. Motherhood was one loss after another.

Claudio dips by the table. "Another Pinot Grigio, Mrs. Vogel?"

"How thoughtful," I say.

"Please." He produces a white saucer with violet olives. "I want you to try these. Just for you."

"You're too kind."

How lovely it is to sit here and think about the past. If no new experience entered my life, I could fill it happily by reliving it. Charles comes late to dinner? I do the puzzle. I look at people. I remember Mr. Wald.

The entomologist was winding up his lepidoptera talk. A voice called, "Yo, Jason!" It was Mr. Wald, the fourth-grade science teacher. "Mr. Wald!" Jason shot out of his seat. "Did you see the silver-bordered fritillary? Did you, Mr. Wald? That's the one I had for Show and Tell."

"Let's check it out." Mr. Wald led Jason by the hand. After a tour of the butterflies, I said, "We're going to the cafeteria for lunch. Care to join us?" While we ate, Jason and Mr. Wald chatted: Was it true touching a butterfly's scales prevented it from flying? The secret to identifying the male monarch. The evolutionary purpose of unjointed false legs. What to feed a caterpillar in captivity. How to avoid wing fade, and on and on, with Mr. Wald glancing up at me and smiling, delighting in Jason's enthusiasm. And the entire time I was unable to speak, not that I chose to. I wanted to revel in the feeling, complete and thorough moltenness. I felt it from my skull to my toes, shocking pleasure. Bolts of it. One after another. Was this what Charles experienced when he looked at porn? Construction workers when they made those kissing sounds in the street? Did men walk around in such a state? The feeling spread through me like a tree. It was brand-new, the center of it right between my legs, with branches that curled around my breasts and unfurled down my legs to my toes. The inside of my elbows. It pulsed my montes.

And then Mr. Wald was getting up and leaning over to . . . *what?* To shake my hand. "Thanks for lunch, Mrs. Vogel." His smile had humor in it! And then he'd called Monday morning, after the boys left on the bus, to thank me again, and he had an insect book for Jason, if I'd care to pick it up. That evening I went to his apartment, knowing if I hadn't I would not be able to be as kind to Charles. I would regret not going to see Mr. Wald to Charles's detriment. If fidelity to Charles prevented me from exploring this feeling, I owed betraying Charles to Charles. I embarked onto Mr. Wald's futon which was too big for us when the queen-size bed I shared with Charles was too small. Accompanying this action was the knowledge: I will be a better wife to Charles if I do not deprive myself because of Charles. I will be a better wife to compensate for my indiscretion. This may be as good as my marriage gets. It is not as good as my life gets.

PRIMO? Yes. PRIMO for BEST. Now. Seven-letter word for INDI-RECT. Starts with O. Not OBSCENE.

And I was able to be more loving to Charles, oddly grateful to him. I was connected to the human history of passion, one of them now. This was what the Song of Solomon and D. H. Lawrence were about. I read Yeats anew. Mr. Wald opened me. OBTRUDE? Nothing less. Was it love? Certainly not. Who was Mr. Wald? My future was with Charles, father of Jason and David. OSMOSIS? OBSCURE? When Mr. Wald moved to Boston for an assistant head-master's job, I was not grieved. If Roberta hadn't seen us stepping out of his walk-up on West Eighteenth Street, that would have been that.

OBLIQUE!

How did Roberta meet her Southern gentleman? Was she able to continue loving Jack? *Die Zauberflöte* has every kind of love: sexual, exalted, divine. Might Yeats have seen it? Yeats was tone-deaf. Does that affect how one hears?

"Look who I found!" Claudio stands in front of the table. His smile makes patrons feel like insiders at a party.

He steadies Charles into a chair. "Whooooa, Mr. Vogel!"

One of the many reasons for Claudio's success is his ability to seat a tipsy husband.

Charles smooches the air in my direction.

"Be a good lad," he says to Claudio even though Claudio is Italian and Charles is not in the Blarney Stone, "and fetch me a double Laphroaig."

If Charles says he's exhausted and must go home, I will go to the opera myself. I will give his ticket to an opera-lover hoping for one at the last minute. I will choose a woman nice to sit next to, someone who won't try to talk to me. An Upper West Side voice coach in a sturdy maroon coat and matching hat who smells like loose face-powder. They are there by the dozen in front of the Met, scanning, ever hopeful.

Ten minutes into the first act, Tamino is lost and Charles is snoring. I elbow him. He clears his throat, opens his eyes. Then his lids sink and he's snoring again. The man in front of us turns around tsking. I squeeze Charles's thigh.

"Charles! 'Die Vogelfanger bin ich ja'! They're playing our song!"

He bolts out of his seat.

"Be right back," he says as Tamino is attacked by the serpent.

"O dass ich doch im Stande wäre" flutters by. Where is Charles? Perhaps ushers won't seat him until intermission. Finally the lights go up. As I enter the aisle, someone grabs my arm.

"Mrs. Vogel?" an usher says.

"Yes?"

"Your husband wasn't feeling well. . . ."

"Yes?"

"He's with the house doctor. I can take you there."

I follow her into the lobby. We turn left. She unlocks a door. This brings us to a dim, boxy green room with a couch. A closed-circuit television broadcasts the gold opera curtain. Papageno's feathers wave as he takes a bow. We pass a glass case with the costume worn by Enrico Caruso in *Pagliacci*. The usher pushes through a hidden door and now we are in a long cinderblock hall with linoleum tiles on the floor and small bleak offices, one after another.

The usher raps a gray metal door. It is opened by a young man in a suit. He raises his eyebrows. "Mrs. Vogel?"

"Yes?"

"I'm Dr. Hernandez. Your husband will be fine."

He looks at me without blinking. How much one can cram in a glance.

"I'm afraid he passed out in the men's room. He has a cut on his chin. It won't require stitches. I used a butterfly Band-Aid."

"I'm sorry." Why am I apologizing?

Dr. Hernandez sweeps a shower curtain aside. The alcove is approximately four by eight. Crutches lean on the wall, along with a collapsible wheelchair and an oxygen tank. Charles snores on a gurney. His tie has been loosened and the first two buttons of his shirt undone. The Band-Aid glows against his stubbled chin.

"Charles!" I shake his arm. "Charles! Wake up! We're going to miss 'Der Holle Rache kocht.' "

"Mrs. Vogel, that's the warning bell."

"Charles!" I pinch the thin skin on the top of his hand. "Please! We love Act Two!"

He snores so deeply his upper lip billows like a sail.

"What should I do, Doctor? He won't wake up."

"I can't leave him alone here, Mrs. Vogel. He's not in any danger, he just had too much to drink. But the rules are, somebody has to stay with him." Then he adds without embarrassment: "I'm a neurology resident, Mrs. Vogel. I never get to go to the opera unless I'm house doc."

"There actually is a doctor in the house?"

"Row CC. On the aisle. Every performance."

"Well go ahead then, Dr. Hernandez," I say. "I can manage."

"If you need me, call my pager." He writes the number down on a Post-it that says Claritin. He starts out the door, then turns around. "Thank you, Mrs. Vogel."

Darn you, Charles. I sit behind the desk. Darn you. I swivel side to side. I scoot in to check him. A string of drool links his mouth to the pillow. I roll back to the desk and test a drawer. Not locked. I open all of them. Tattered *Playboys*, Styrofoam cups, a watch cap, condoms, a fossilized half-donut, pencils, a navy muffler. A stainless-steel trolley corrals glass jars of tongue depressors and cotton swabs. There's a box of rubber gloves that pop up like Kleenex.

The doctor should have stayed with Charles. I pluck a handful of rubber gloves and stuff them in my bag. It is the house doctor's job and he was given a free ticket and Charles pays a fortune for our subscription. The doctor is here for an exchange of services. Missing two acts is an occupational hazard. What if Charles were to choke? The doctor was kind though. He did not look at me slyly or worse, with pity. He said thank you. I cram the gloves back in the box.

On the trolley there is a tray with scissors doctors use to cut adhesive tape, scissors with blades like duck bills that slide beneath. I go in to Charles. I slip them under a hank of hair behind his left ear. Charles has magnificent hair. I cut it off as close as I can get, one square inch.

After the final curtain, Dr. Hernandez returns. He wrestles Charles into the wheelchair and rolls him to the curb. Opera-lovers surge past the fountain, then disperse into the night, disappearing into limos, buses, subways, and cabs. Dr. Hernandez stays with us until we get a taxi. Helping us in, he thanks me again.

"One ten Riverside Drive." I buckle us up.

. . .

Our doorman checks the window. "Good evening, Mrs. Vogel." He opens the door. He helps me hoist Charles to the elevator.

"Thank you, Jimmy."

We stumble into the boys' old room. I help Charles onto Jason's bed. I unlace his shoes, peel off his suit, remove his wallet and keys. I check the breast pocket of his jacket. There is a folded piece of paper in it, a yellow brochure. I open it. *Recovery Groups for Men with Controlling Partners*, it says.

13 · T the P

Sure I thought about it. What wife doesn't? But I never did it. Did you cheat on me, Fred? I know what you'd say if I asked. "Why would I want another woman, Nans? I can't stand the one I've got." No. You'd laugh and say, "If you can think of it, it can happen." If we had a coat of arms, "If you can think of it, it can happen," would be appliquéd in gold.

Fred unfaithful? I don't want that thought in my house.

If I had a lover would I have told Bobbie? Only if I wanted the world to know.

If I had a lover would I want Flora to know after I'm dead? No way. Not if I'd had the lover when Freddy was alive. Looking at family photos, she'd see something new in every one. She'd have to rethink her childhood. Knowing I'd been unfaithful to her father would undermine her past.

What if Alice tells Betsy?

Did Jack know?

I'm glad she didn't tell me while she was alive. If I'd known, how would I have faced him? It's rotten knowing something about someone that person doesn't know you know. There are three kinds of secrets. Your own. The secrets people tell you. And discovered secrets, ones you wish you didn't have.

I put up decaf and read the letter again. "My" book? He was the author? The book belonged to him?

Interesting she'd be friends with both of us. Alice and I have zilch in common. Getting her to help was like pulling teeth. Impacted wisdom teeth. What did Bobbie like about her? Does everybody have different friends for different things? I have colleagues who are friends of proximity. Neighbors from the building I wouldn't be friends with if they didn't live in the building. Book-club friends I never see outside book club. Friends for tennis in the park.

What kind of friend was Bobbie? We couldn't go to museums. She talked in front of pictures. There you'd be, lost in a painting or a sculpture, and she'd be blabbing her brains out, ruining it. "The Standing Woman's name was Isabel Dutaud Nagle. She was ten years older than Gaston Lachaise. It took him seven years to talk her out of her clothes. She came from Boston. He first saw her standing on a bridge in Paris." And Bobbie hated going to museums with me. "You know what you are?" she'd say. "You're a Museum Martinet."

I can go to museums with Jill, but I can't eat in a restaurant with her. "Is the pastrami fatty or lean? Is the coleslaw made with vine-gar or mayo? This coffee doesn't taste fresh. Could you make another pot? Could you fill my cup to the brim?"

Dana can keep a secret and, better yet, knows when to shut up about it. As opposed to Carol, who brought things up long after they'd been buried. If a child failed a math test in the third grade, when the kid was a senior, Carol would still be asking in a sad, wor-ried voice, "How is poor so-and-so doing in math?" No one was better when you were home with the flu.

Bobbie had a special place. We brainstormed challenging cases. She was a gifted therapist. We loved each other's daughters. We took trips. I was my funniest with Bobbie. We'd crack up in the chemo room. Was that everybody's experience with her? She saw me the way I hoped I was. Did Ice Maiden laugh with her too?

I fold up the letter and put it back in my bag. What if Bobbie didn't have a plan? Some people do things, they don't know why. A therapist sees that hourly. Especially dealing with children. Some-thing will make itself clear. I'll just have to trust the process. "T the P," as Bobbie would say.

. . .

The man across the way is home. He goes out less than I do. Why does a man wear a shower cap in his living room? Does he color his hair? Would I recognize him on the street? Maybe we pass each other every day. What a pain, having to see him. Bobbie's solution: "Take a curtain rod, buy a pashmina. Not one of those eight-hundred-dollar ones. You won't have to wait long. When they get really cheap, buy one and fling it over the rod. Cover the OPW, leaving only the trees."

Bobbie tracked what she called the Pashmina Fad Infiltration Index. "Goat-wattle hair has taken over the world," she said. "We are at the mercy of Himalayan goat-wattle hair. This is a genuine cross-all-lines fad. It's the Nehru jacket, the Courrèges boot, the Ali MacGraw *Love Story* watch cap of the nineties."

After that conversation, she began charting pashmina prog-ress. "You can get one for six hundred at Barney's!" she'd say. Or "Look, a two-for-one in the *Times!*" "Now they're at the Limited!" "Kmart's got 'em!" Eventually, she said, people will wrap fish in them.

Pashmina Alert was contagious. It got so, every time we saw a woman shrink-wrapped in pashmina, we'd hold our sides. We walked New York on Full Pashmina Alert. "Let's wait till they pay us to take them," she said. Finally they were at the Dollar Tree.

Alice Vogel, Sourpuss Extraordinaire. A woman without laugh lines. Her lips bend down at the corners, like Joan Crawford's. If Bobbie were alive, she'd give me a list of turned-down-mouth beauties. Bette Davis. Katharine Hepburn. Jeanne Moreau. Today lips no longer go down. They're puffy, plumped with collagen, autologous fat, AlloDerm, Restalyne, and silicone. Today beauty is the fat lip, the Battered Lip Look, as if women had taken a hard left straight from the shoulder, bruised into submission. Jeez. What next? The Bloody Nose Look? The Black Eye? If Bobbie were alive, she'd be the only person I could call with this. She'd get it. We marched for choice and women are choosing to look like victims? Why aren't our kids marching? I want Flora to march. Doesn't she know she can change the world?

Did I know Bobbie well enough to figure this out? When was that conversation we had? Not that long after you died, Freddy. So it had to be less than three years ago. We'd seen a movie together, something where two unlikely people were thrust together, and the audience knows before the people on the screen know, they'll wind up churning sheets. You wait contentedly for it. You were newly dead then, Fred. Afterward, over coffee, I said: "Bobbie. Tell me the truth. Think I'll ever have that wild, going-to-hell-in-a-handbasket, obsessional, skid-on-the-floor, crash-on-the-bed, wall-thumping, pictures-fall-on-your-head, fuck-me, fuck-me, fuck-me-till-I'm-blue, I-don't-care, I-don't-care, crazy, greedy lust for a man again?"

And she said, "If you do, run the other way."

How the hell can I do this myself?

I get out of bed and head for the little room.

From: nannypoo@aol.com
To: Luba1102@earthlink.com
Subject: mystery man
Dear Alice,
I really think we need to get together one more
time. Whatever has to be done, she wanted both
of us to do it. How about lunch any day next
week, same place?
Warmly, Nanny

We need. The language of cooperation.

I click out of AOL and the desktop pops up. The Civil War nut must be from the South. Who did Bobbie know from the South? Her roommate at Cornell was from the South. Janie Something. She was at the funeral. Janie Pirelli? Janie Goodyear? Janie *Good-*

rich from Charleston who married that guy in the journalism school. A writer. They kept moving all over the country. Bobbie had dinner with them when they came to New York. Is that who he is? Janie's husband?

I Google "White Pages" and check "Jane Goodrich." She could have kept her maiden name.

Eight Jane Goodriches show up.

Bobbie thought he was a genius. Every time he had something in *The Nation,* she e'd it to me. What was his name again? Oscar? Oliver? *Owen!* Owen *what?*

This is impossible.

Wait a minute. *The Nation.*

I Google "The Nation." Now what? "The Nation–Jane Goodrich." Nothing. I try "The Nation–Owen." Owen Achs! Achs! Right! Now what?

Google "Owen Achs."

He's not the Icelandic sculptor.

He's not a purveyor of flat-head nails.

But he is, most likely, the reporter at the *St. Petersburg Times.*

Let's see where he lives.

Tallahassee. Was Tallahassee in the Civil War?

I type in "White Pages." Then "Achs." Then "Tallahassee" and "FL."

"Owen Achs" and "Jane Achs." Two numbers.

I dial the Jane number. A woman's voice says, "You know what to do and you know when to do it."

I leave a message after the beep:

"This is Nanny Wunderlich. I'm Bobbie Bloom's friend? We had dinner in New York a gazillion years ago and I saw you again at the funeral. Please call me at 212 572-2593."

14 · Pleasure You Can Count On

When the only individual who knows your secret dies, two changes occur. You lose the sole person you can discuss your secret with. That and: your secret is safe.

Roberta did not have secrets. Except the one. Two, counting mine. Roberta was missing—how to say?—a respect for privacy? Fear of being judged? Shame? When Betsy was suspended from school for sneaking a boy into the girls' locker room, Roberta laughed and told everyone. She refused to use the traditional New York suspension cover story: "Betsy's home with mono." When Jack drove his Saab out of the showroom and demolished it three minutes later on the West Side Highway, Roberta burnished it into a set piece. You simply could not tell Roberta a thing. Betrayals started with "Alice. You gotta swear you won't tell I told you," or "Promise you won't repeat this?," or "I was sworn to secrecy but I can tell you." When she was in treatment, she announced it to the world:

"Do you have this in a smaller size? I'm getting chemo."

"Is this a Limited bus? By the way, I have cancer."

"Can you get the cleaning to me Wednesday, Joe? I might not be here Thursday."

I, on the other hand, treasure secrets. I will take Mr. Wald to the grave. Should my mammogram be bad next month, I will tell Charles and Charles alone. I will not inform the boys. And because of that, their wives' mothers will not call forlorn and say, "Oh Alice, you poor dear, how *are* you?" as if one owed them a medical update. There would be no one on my death watch. I would not have to hear cancer stories about people worse off that are meant

87

to cheer. Or the opposite, stories about women "who sailed right through," as if any other woman's experience had relevance. People you barely know asking for details as if cancer made you public domain. People who want to know because you make them feel lucky. Or people who, once they knew, stared at your head to see if your hair was falling out or sneaked looks at your breasts to check if they could tell which one. People who used the word "sick." Sick is a cold. It would sink me to hear, "You're in our prayers."

Best of all, I will not have to hear the most meaningless words in the universe:

"I know you're going to be okay."

You do?

Would I have been able to hide it from Roberta? We scheduled our mammograms together. Who will take me to my mammogram now that I don't have Roberta? How can she not be here?

No, I would not have told Roberta. Secrets are allies. I would not have told her about Mr. Wald either. Yes, she saw us. I can only hope that for me, her oldest friend, she honored my privacy.

And now it appears Charles has secrets too. What was that exercise in *Recovery Groups for Men with Controlling Partners*? "Name the three most abusive things your partner has done." Regardless how abusive the partner was, one had to work at this, narrow it to three. Once the three most egregious events were established, the man had to face his partner and say what they were. There would be a surprise or two on both sides.

A pity beyond all telling
Is hid in the heart of love

Surely I would know were Charles unhappy. Does setting him up in the boys' room constitute abuse? When Charles requested I stop editing his closet, did I not do so immediately? When he mentioned his bad cholesterol, Häagen-Dazs coffee—my favorite— was expunged for sorbet. Would I ever take my hair down were it not to please Charles? I suspect there is a double standard of sorts. But in the end, it is a healthy double standard. Charles pinning me to the mattress. His final breathy "Loveya" consistent since our wedding night. The rest of the week doing what he's done throughout our married life, masturbating, originally to magazines, now that video he stashes behind the VCR. How many times have I stumbled on him in flagrante, his navy sweatpants telescoped around his calves? Is masturbation in a marriage a good thing? According to the *Times*, the percentage of single men who admit to masturbating once a week or more is 48. Percentage of married men: 44. Percentage of men with graduate degrees: 80. Percentage of men who never finished college: 52. Percentage of men under fifty who've thought about sex in the last five minutes: 87. Over fifty, 48.

Over sixty? Sex researchers do not research over sixty.

Charles is a sixty-three-year-old married man with a law degree who masturbates to *Cumming in America*.

I unpack dinner. Roberta used to say, "Home cooking is anything purchased within six blocks of your apartment." I am serving my husband the world's healthiest meal: salmon, broccoli, and sweet potatoes. Nothing carcinogenic. If, that is, the potatoes actually are organic. If the salmon was, indeed, not farm-raised and the broccoli rabe not bio-engineered. I am either poisoning us or boosting our immune systems.

I set the table with gray linen and white Wedgwood. Food will be the color. I put the kettle on and hang up my clothes. I pull a djellabah over my head. It is raw silk the color of platinum, dupioni spun by twin caterpillars in the same cocoon. I undo my watch and place it on the semainier. The gray lizard band against the mahogany is exquisite. So many pleasures are accidental. The way a pink-lined lampshade funnels light against the wall. A Charles James "La Sirène" buried in a derelict valise dropped off at the store. A watery-green silk duvet atop starched white sheets. There is much pleasure in these sheets. Predictable pleasure. Pleasure you can count on.

What could Charles find abusive? Have I ever, in thirty-eight years, denied him? I adore sex. Even his, rubbing that could wake the dead. Must redefining pleasure negate the pleasure of the past? If I thought our sex was fine, does the knowledge of better sex make it less so? If you loved Leni Riefenstahl's *Blue Light* when you saw it, do you suddenly hate it when you learn it was Hitler's favorite movie?

The kettle whistles. Let's see. Green tea? Too much caffeine. Linden leaves, *tilleul*, Proust's tea. Perfect for *Moby-Dick* and "the white curdling cream of the squall." While it steeps, I call Charles to remind him about dinner.

"How was your day?" he asks.

"Wonderful, Charles. And yours?"

"I may get a client from Rakower."

"Charles!"

"It's a property division, but at least I'm on his screen. Alice?"

"Yes, Charles?"

"I owe you an opera."

"I know you'll make good on it, dear."

"I'm sorry, Alice."

"See you at eight, Charles. I made something you'll like."

When the tea is ready, I slip a cozy on to keep it warm. It's printed with a black-and-white etching of a pig. Am I becoming one of those women—yes, I may very well be—who take great joy making a perfect cup of tea? What next? Alphabetizing the herbs? Putting ribbons round the linens?

I check my date book to see if I've accomplished everything. Once when Jason was still in the perambulator, I pushed him to the park. It was a beautiful day, the first sunny afternoon of a protracted winter. We were meeting Roberta and Betsy. The sailing pond was teeming with toddlers scrambling over Hans Christian

Andersen. I squeezed in between a nanny and an elderly gentle-man with a white mustache and black homburg. After a few min-utes taking in the sun, he reached into the breast pocket of his chesterfield and produced a thin black book. He began flipping the pages. From the corner of my eye it was possible to see all of them were blank except for two entries repeated at regular intervals: HAIR and TEETH.

Could that ever be me?

I pour a cup of pale *tilleul*. It looks exquisitely anemic against the blue-white Sèvres. After Roberta saw me on his stoop, she wanted me to know she had a Mr. Wald too? Yes, that might be it. Then why bring her other friend into it? Perhaps Nanny had a secret friend as well.

I make myself comfortable on the living-room couch and find my place in *Moby-Dick*. I close my eyes for a moment.

"Hey."

I must have dozed off. "Hey to you, Charles."

He busses my cheek.

"What time is it?"

"Nine-thirty. Had to meet Rakower for a drink."

"Ah."

"I had a ginger ale, Alice."

Hardly my business. I've raised children. I have no intention of raising a husband. How could Charles possibly see me as a "con-trolling partner." Am I still his girl?

"Am I still your girl?"

"Yup. Still my girl."

"Give me a kiss," I say.

"Get up." Charles extends a hand.

I put my book down and swing my legs off the couch. Charles places his left arm around my waist and pushes my right shoulder toward the floor. He is dipping me for his Rhett Butler extravaganza. I keep my eyes open. His face gets closer. Gray tusklike hairs curl out of his nostrils. Thousands of dark pores constellate his nose. He smiles, and I notice his lowers overlap like carelessly shuffled cards. When did that happen?

Charles laughs. If smell had form and color, I would be enveloped in a puce haze the size of a hassock. Yet underneath his layers of imposed scent—aftershave, the remains of lunch—I smell my Charles, the waxy, wet-wool, raw-potato Charles smell. I close my eyes. He kisses me on the forehead.

15 · Hard-Wired for Love

A woman in a long black cape speedwalks up Madison. She's walking so fast, the cape inflates, and I think, *Bobbie!* It's almost a month and this morning I woke up thinking: *Gotta call Bobbie!*

Jeez, I wish she was here, checking this out with me. The apartment is that prewar six on Ninety-seventh and Fifth. In ad speak, "A Classic 6." It has two bedrooms, a dining room, kitchen, living room, and a "little room" or "home office," a "back room," what used to be "the maid's."

"Lookee here, Nans!" Bobbie'd open a closet. "Eight identical pairs of black Ferragamo flats? Either she teaches at a girls' school or she's taller than her husband." In a medicine chest filled with vintage perfume bottles: "Uh-oh, eBay addict." A pantry stocked with Maalox, Metamucil, and Tagament: "Somebody works on Wa-a-a-all Street!" she'd sing.

I start my first walk-through. "Fifth Avenue Classic 6," the ad forms in my head. Not that anything's classic about a classic six. A classic six can have rooms enfilade or scatter-shot. Pantry, no pantry. Walk-in closets, closets like coffins.

"Fifth Avenue Classic 6." The building may be on Fifth, but it's north of Ninety-sixth, so it'll go for half the identical apartment two blocks south. Will it be right for the Glogowers? Will it put them out of their misery? I want them to be happy. Steve waited tables in law school. They remind me of us thirty years ago.

"Fifth Avenue Classic 6." Too bad it's in the back. It's darker than Smokey Joe's Cafe, and any half-wit reading the ad will know it has no views or the ad would lead with "Fab Park Vus."

"Fifth Avenue Classic 6! Wake up with Central Park Outside Your Door!" Now that's true. Central Park is outside your *lobby* door.

"Fifth Avenue Classic 6! Wake up with Central Park Outside Your Door! Windowed Kitchen!" How many people would call to see a place if the ad read "Six Room Dungeon! Brick Wall Vu! Troglodyte Kitchen!" Not that it won't wind up some family's dream apartment. Once people mortgage their lives for a co-op, it becomes their Eden. They visit friends with park views and think, *All that light! How can they stand it?* They praise their non-furniture-fading darkness and count their blessings they can't hear garbage trucks. It is a well-known New York co-op truth that once a family goes into hock for an apartment, that's the best apartment there is.

Not that this one has no virtues. It's across from a playground. The little room could be a third bedroom or home office. If the buyers break down the wall between the little room and the kitchen, they'll have what New York calls a "California kitchen."

"Fifth Avenue Classic 6! Wake up with Central Park Outside Your Door! Windowed Kitchen! Home Office Potential!"

Last week, I showed the Glogowers an apartment with a gift-wrapping center. The seller had taken the door off a pantry, and now a three-walled nave was devoted to the pursuit of the perfectly wrapped box. Rows of gold and silver paper, Happy Birthday! It's a Boy! It's a Girl! It's Conjoined Twins! Rainbows of ribbons on cardboard spools and racks of little cards, like the florist's. There are lives in which the wrapping of a gift is important enough to merit fifty square feet of prime New York real estate. That's $150,000 on the open market. How long before a buyer comes along and says, "You know, that gift-wrapping center would make a dandy pantry! Hey, I got an idea! Let's put up a door!"

If I could tell this to Bobbie, she'd be on the floor.

That eight on Park with the third bedroom converted to a

closet, the clothes on remote-controlled dry-cleaner rods. Once I opened a linen closet and a man was in there typing.

Lord, these rooms are tiny. Excuse me, "cozy."

Place is a wreck. Excuse me, "pristine."

"Fifth Avenue Classic 6! Wake up with Central Park Outside Your Door! Windowed Kitchen! Home Office Potential! Original Prewar Condition!" Let's say we get one-four for it. Six percent of one-four is eighty-four thousand. Split that with Gabriella Sinclair-Gault and it's forty-two. Split that with Jeanette for giving me the listing and I've grossed twenty-one. Before taxes. If we get the asking price. I sell three like this a year, I'm cool. I don't have to pillage Fred's TIAA-CREF crumbs. Three apartments a year plus Social Security on the horizon. Sounds like a plan.

I pick up a pound of mixed fish, garlic for the aioli, and a French bread. Flora likes those brown-sugar cupcakes from Yura. Should I tell her about the letter? No way. She loved her Aunt Bobbie. She'd have to keep it from Betsy or, worse, tell. I'm glad I was faithful if for no other reason than I don't have to lie to my daughter.

Why didn't I invite Betsy for dinner too? Flora was so prickly about her last week. Will their friendship survive? Now that they're not pushed together by Bobbie and me? They're as unalike or the same as any two strangers. The two of them were my master's thesis, my living laboratory for a study on innate temperament.

Betsy slept hard, content from Day One. She welcomed the playpen. If Bobbie put on Bach, Betsy stared at the ceiling for hours. A calm baby. But such a picky eater.

And Floradorable? We thought we'd go nuts. A nap-rejecter. Fearless Flora, who at nine months climbed out of her crib and showed up laughing in the bedroom. Scared the hell out of us. Florapie, who drained an eight-ounce bottle nonstop, breathing like a trombone player. The first eighteen years of their lives, those girls did everything together. Sand box, schools, camp. Will they stay friends? I can't make it happen, but I'd like Floradorable to have one friend in life as good as Bobbie. Two girls without sibs, witnesses to each other's childhoods. That isn't enough?

At home, I lay everything out on the counter then ditch my suit. Free again. It's a miracle getting into this old bathtub hasn't killed me. It requires full focus, all my physical and mental faculties, the sides are that high. Should I get one of those clutches? Grippers? *Grabber bars.*

"Yo, Ma!" Flora gives me a kiss.

She drags her finger through the brown-sugar buttercream, leaving a track, ruining it, spoiling her appetite. My mother would have slapped my hand away, but what's the point. I'm glad Flora's here. This cupcake was purchased to please her.

She plops on the stepstool and chomps a carrot. She's wearing low-cut jeans. A tee shirt advertises her coccyx. No tattoos. No pierces I can see. They gave us the wrong baby, Freddy. Somewhere there's a girl with curly brown hair and big hips.

Flora is describing an incident at work. Some tale with good guys and bad guys and dumb guys and smart guys, all of whom are women, and it occurs to me that poaching fish in my kitchen with my daughter yakking is one of life's great pleasures.

"What?"

"You never listen to me, Ma," she says.

"I always listen to you, Floradora."

"You space-travel, Ma. You go blank. *Zonk.*"

"I heard every word you said."

"Okay. Tell me. What did I say?"

"Well, maybe I was daydreaming. But I was daydreaming about you."

"I hate when you do that."

"Okay, honey. You were saying?"

"Now I forgot."

"Flora?"

"Yes?"

"Do you miss Aunt Bobbie?"

"Truth?"

"No. Lie to me."

"I'm sorry your best friend is dead, Ma. But Aunt Bobbie, sometimes she was hard to take."

"You loved her!"

"*You* loved her. She had this level of . . . *cheeriness*. She was always so . . . so *positive*."

"What my generation calls 'upbeat.' "

"Well my generation calls it 'manic' and 'manipulative.' Why did she have to be upbeat when I had chicken pox? Why was she cheery when Sam broke up with me? When Bets and I had a fight?"

"I thought you loved being with her."

"*You* loved being with her. You *chose* when to be with her."

"Oh, sweetheart."

"There were good things too, Mom. I could do no wrong. She taught me to whistle."

"We're invited to Uncle Jack's next week, you know."

"Do I have to go?"

"Betsy will be there, honey. You haven't seen her since the funeral."

"You keep throwing us together, Mom."

"I do?"

"Always. Then you tell her how proud you are of her. Admit it, Ma. You think less of me because I didn't go to Columbia."

"I couldn't care less where you went. You and Betsy have so much in common."

"You and Daddy would have liked an academic."

"That again? Come here and stir this for me, will you?"

While she wilts the onions, she tells me about the man she ran into she used to go to school with. The man she met in a bar who sent flowers the next day. The man she recently broke up with but still loves only not that way anymore who is going to a therapist twice a week which Flora feels sure will help him grow, even if he grows for the next woman. The man she sat next to on a plane flying back from a business trip in Los Angeles who—what? I'm not sure I'm hearing this right, she talks faster than the speed of sound—who invited her to join the Mile High Club? What will Flora's daughter someday tell her she won't want to hear? If this is what Flora tells me, what doesn't she tell me? Does Flora have secrets? Does she carry condoms? Her generation sleeps with men first, *then* gets to know them. Could I do that, someone hardwired for love?

"Teddy and I are going out again."

I pour in white wine and clam juice.

"Teddy? When I was growing up, exes hated each other. You'd cross the street if you saw them coming."

"That's awful, Ma," Flora says. "You don't just stop caring about someone. Want me to make the salad?"

Before I can say no, she jumps off the stool and starts slamming cabinets. Control yourself, Nanny. A whole tin of anchovies opened for one anchovy. A new Parmesan started when there's plenty on the old rind. Spills, sprays, open cans in the fridge, "Where's this? Where's that?" A small price to pay for time with my girl.

"Mom." She studies my yogurts. "These expired in August."

"Yogurt doesn't go bad."

"It's *December.*"

"Flora, you know I hate waste."

"I'm tossing these, Mom. Gross."

She chucks my Parmesan rind too. Out go the bendable carrots that would have been fine in a soup.

"How old are these eggs? I want the truth!" She scrutinizes the side of the carton. "Mom! You're why they invented dates on food."

The eggs go in the trash, followed by all the ice creams with snow under the lid. You only have to scrape the snow. Snow protects ice cream like skin on a pudding. She grabs an open bottle of red I was going to add to the vinegar.

"Put that back this minute." I wrestle her. "It's cheaper to buy you dinner than have you mug my fridge."

She starts in on a head of romaine. She pulls off so many outer leaves, she's left with a miniature white torpedo. "Mom," she says, "we need more romaine."

She drains a can of chickpeas and runs water in the can, not to dirty the colander. She shakes the can until the chickpeas are rinsed. Good. She's learned something from me.

"Mom," she says, "you know my friend Dahlia from work?"

"The Israeli girl in the art department?"

"Her parents are divorced and we were talking. We want to set you up with her father."

"An Israeli?"

"Her mother's from Israel. He's from New York."

"You want us to go on a date?"

"It's no big deal, Mom. Do what you tell me. Meet him for coffee."

"Have you met him?"

"Uh-huh. He takes Dahlia to dinner every Tuesday."

"What's he like?"

She points to her head with the garlic press. "More hair than Daddy."

When you're pushing sixty and you sleep with a man for the first time, do you turn out the lights? If you leave the lights on, do you pull your nightgown down from your shoulders or raise it from the hem? Do you want him to see your breasts first or your stomach? Can you leave your nightgown on? The thought of being undressed in front of a new man, a new man taking me in. When I looked at Freddy, I saw him the way he was in the present and the how he used to be. Both at once. Who was it that said, People get married so there's one less naked person to see.

"Everybody has more hair than Daddy," I say.

"He's not fat. He's not tall. He's not short. I like him. Say yes, Mom."

"Sure," I say. "Give him my number. Coffee? I'd meet Godzilla for coffee."

16 · Dinner with a Belly Surgeon

Nanny stands outside the door. She raises her arm to ring the bell. Light bounces off her bracelet:

ALLERGIC TO FISH
WEARING CONTACT LENSES

She wonders if Bobbie's black cape will still be in the hall closet, if her books still line the dining room. Will they eat there, where the hospital bed had been?

She rings. Nanny has not been in the apartment since the funeral November 6. When her husband died, the week after the funeral Nanny donated his black La-Z-Boy to the super. She called the Salvation Army to evacuate the shoe-polishing machine, StairMaster, treadmill, and weights. The lumpy tweed jackets he taught in, the navy blazer that hadn't buttoned since Kennedy. Her husband believed a blazer was a blazer for life. When it no longer buttoned, it was worn open. Later, when it got big again, he'd drape it over his shoulders like a yachtsman. Their daughter said no to all of it, taking only a herringbone newsboy cap and black Persian Envoy, hats she grew up with, hats older than she was.

Jack answers the door. "Nanny!"

He gives her his antiseptic doctor's hug, pushing away as it holds. She looks toward the living room. Nothing appears different, except on the piano a photo of Bobbie.

"Oh, Jack."

"Don't," he says. "Makes it worse."

Nanny follows him into the kitchen. On the way, she passes the bookcases. The books are every which way, scraps of paper poking out, well-used books, much loved. Nanny thinks about the line from the letter: ". . . and spend the evening reading my book to you . . ."

"Auntie Nanny!" Betsy nestles, softly familiar, in Nanny's arms.

Nanny rubs Betsy's back in circles. It is the same motion she used burping the girls thirty years ago.

Flora salutes with a wooden spoon.

"Smells great!" Nanny says, and dips a pita chip into hummus. She recognizes the bowl. Bobbie bought it on one of their trips. Jack stayed in the hotel reading. He'd bought *Death in Venice* to read in Venice while Bobbie, Freddy and Nanny took a vaporetto to Murano. They watched the bowl being made. It was the color of a full sour pickle shot with gold sparkles and shaped like a lily. It cost over two hundred dollars then. Bobbie had to have it.

"We made the same bowl for Mussolini." The salesman smiled, swiping her credit card.

When Bobbie showed Jack Mussolini's bowl, he said, "Take it back. How could you?"

And Bobbie said, "Mussolini's dead. The bowl is beautiful."

"Not beautiful enough," Jack said.

For Jack a wartime enemy was an enemy for life. He refused to drink Sapporo beer or buy a Sony Walkman. An Audi was out of the question. Everywhere Jack went, he scouted the Running Man. Swastikas on ski sweaters, pottery of ancient Greece, tesserae floor borders. An awning on East Sixty-third Street. Chinese rugs. The frieze at 1040 Fifth. Jack was on the case, a Swastika Detective. He pointed them out in Rome and the elevators of the Carlyle. Bobbie laughed each time. "Good for you, Jack, honey," she roared. "Another trophy for the Stika Dicka!" And here was Mussolini's bowl.

"Wine, Mom?" Flora sashays over with a bottle of red. A

U-shaped apron, the kind French maids wore in Depression-era comedies, is tied over her jeans.

The women help. Jack slices five Yukon Golds into waxy rounds, then overlaps them in circles on a platter.

Flora minces parsley. "It looks like a camellia, Uncle Jack."

Nanny tackles the vinaigrette.

Betsy crumbles blue cheese over the platter like pixie dust.

The doorbell rings.

"I'll get it." Betsy races to the door.

"Aunt Alice." She wraps herself around Alice Vogel.

"Darling," Alice says.

Nanny ventures out of the kitchen. She observes them holding each other.

Betsy looks up. "You remember Mom's friend, Alice Vogel? From my birthday parties?"

"Sure. You bet," Nanny says. "How've you been?"

"Nice to see you, Nanny." A smile escapes. "After all these years."

While Jack grills sausages, Nanny plots a way to check the books. She is convinced a lover with a passion would want to share that passion.

Nibbling a celery stick, Alice studies Jack, how easily he moves between the sink and the stove. She tries to picture Roberta performing the ancillary work duplicity requires. It is not possible to envision Roberta skulking.

Nanny watches Alice watch Jack. She is certain her late husband would have known if she'd been having an affair.

Both women know things about Jack he does not know they know, things their friend told them. Both women think about them now. They know Jack had been kicked by a horse when he was nine and had an orchiectomy. They know his father threw his allowance on the floor, forcing Jack to crawl around for it. Both know Jack has to turn the water on to urinate. A belly surgeon, "a man who holds pulsing guts in his hands," can't go without hearing the rush of water. They know that sometimes when Jack opens a patient up, he sobs in the OR. The nurses pat his tears with gauze pads. They know when Jack travels he takes the Fussus Mussus, his childhood teddy bear. They know he holds a grudge, fans it, never forgets an insult. He has a Nixon's List of people who have double-crossed him, not been on his side, said things about him behind his back. But most of all, there is the man who threw his allowance on the floor. Their friend used to say a man abused by his father is always waiting to be injured. Especially by the person supposed to love him. Injury is what he knows. That's what love is to him.

According to their friend, none of this made Jack less desirable. "I've got a list of women who'll be lining up with hot casseroles," she said after making the decision to stop treatment. "Watch. The day the notice goes in the *Times,* that night the doorbell will ring. You'll see. A stampede of grief-stricken women loaded with potted meatballs and lasagna. A solvent single doctor with an apartment? They'd take him sight-unseen."

Neither woman is particularly fond of Jack. He was Roberta's husband. When the couples took vacations, Jack preferred reading to visiting caiman farms, single-malt breweries, and bell foundries. Both women think of Jack as a package deal, the man who came with their friend. The man who would tell you the right doctor to go to if you asked.

"I think we're ready," Jack announces.

They parade platters to the table.

So many books, Nanny thinks. If there is a book on the Civil War, what if it's dedicated "To My Darling Bobbie"?

"This is absolutely lovely." Alice turns to Jack.

"You guys did a great job," Nanny says.

Alice wonders: Do Nanny and Jack worry about their daughters? They should have been married years ago. If Betsy and Jason had married, he'd be living in New York now.

Nanny wonders: How can Alice stand it? Two boys on the coast? What if Flora moved to the coast? I'd have to move to a culture where women scoop the insides out of bagels to save a calorie.

"Bobbie thought you were a great cook, Nanny," Jack says. "And Alice, she thought you ordered in with the best of them."

Her name on the table. That easy. "I adored the way she cooked," Alice says. "Especially her meatloaf."

"Dad made the meatloaf," Betsy says.

"Then I loved her beet salad."

"Didn't Mom get that from Citarella, Dad?"

Alice wonders if she ever tasted anything Roberta made.

Nanny looks at Jack's heavy shoulders straining against his white shirt. She thinks, If Jack and I fell in love, our girls would be sisters. I'd have *two* daughters. Studying Jack, she feels no inclination to know him a different way. She decides if she finagles everybody else into doing the dishes, she can get to the bookshelves.

"I haven't seen you since the funeral," Betsy is saying to Flora.

"You girls." Nanny snaps to. "You live twenty-one blocks from each other."

"Auntie Nanny," Betsy says, "that's an ocean."

"It's an M7 bus, sweetheart."

Betsy hurls a laugh. It is her mother's laugh.

Nanny decides to find out about Owen Achs.

"Wasn't that Janie Goodrich at the funeral? I haven't seen her in twenty years."

"Roberta's old roommate from college," Alice adds. "I thought I recognized her."

"Poor Janie." Jack shakes his head.

"What happened?" Alice asks.

"Owen was teaching journalism at FSU. You knew that."

"I knew he was a writer," Alice says.

"He married a student. Had twins."

"Jeez," Nanny says.

"Owen's grandchildren are older than his children."

"If Dad were alive," Flora says, "and you guys divorced? I'd be miserable if he subdivided his love."

"I'd hate if you had more kids," Betsy addresses her father.

"So would I," Jack says.

"I want you to be happy, Dad. But I like being your only child. Is that selfish?"

"Imagine, Jack," Alice says. "The rigors of child-rearing in your sixties."

Nanny pictures bending down a thousand times a day to pick up red and yellow Legos.

"And a twenty-four-year-old wife. That's what did it," Jack says.

"Did what, Uncle Jack?"

"Owen had an aneurysm. You didn't know? Died like Rockefeller."

"What a thing," Nanny says. "Without Rockefeller, we wouldn't have the Adirondack Park. And that's what he'll be remembered for, dying in the saddle with his sweetie pie."

"Was he hounded like President Clinton?" Flora asks.

"It's hard to hound a dead man," Jack replies. "People talked. The story got around. But nobody talked about Roosevelt, Ike, or Kennedy. Everybody knew but nobody talked about it."

"That wasn't how you sold papers then," Nanny adds.

"Politicians were permitted a private life," Alice says.

"A private life or secret life?" Betsy asks.

The table goes quiet.

"I mean"—Betsy runs her fingers through her spiky blond hair—"there's a difference between something private and something secret, isn't there?" Her eyes leap from person to person.

"Hmmmm," Nanny dives in. "Well, I suppose a secret is something you want to hide, need to hide, maybe for self-preservation. And something private, well that's just nobody else's business."

"I think of a secret as something that has the potential to hurt someone," Alice says. "It could hurt the teller of the secret or the person the secret is about. Whereas something private is something that cannot affect any life other than one's own. Something private has no moral implication. It does not require dissemination."

"Give an example," Jack says.

Alice thinks. "All right, Jack. Here. Were I to murder Charles by grinding twenty Ambien into his applesauce, that would be a secret. But if Charles killed himself by grinding twenty Ambien into his applesauce, that would be private."

Betsy pinks with excitement. "Secrets are things you're ashamed of," she says. "Private things are things that get diluted if you share them."

"Give an example," Flora says.

"Okay. If I falsified research on my Debussy thesis, that would be my secret. But if a man I loved said something wonderful to me, that would be so very private. What do you think, Flor?"

"Private is something no one else has a right to know. Private means you have boundaries, things that are off-limits to talk about. A secret is something you're hiding from other people. I agree with Alice. A secret is something that could hurt you if other people knew."

"You may have to lie to keep a secret," Alice adds. "But you needn't lie to keep something private."

"A provocative dichotomy," Jack says.

Nanny pushes her chair from the table. "The buck stops with your dictionary."

"I know where it is," Betsy says. She goes straight to the reference shelf and hands *Webster's* to Nanny.

Nanny riffles. ". . . Prissy," she says. ". . . Prithee . . . Ah." She places her index finger on a word. She reads for a moment. "Get this: 'Private' has five meanings, and number five is 'Secret,' as in 'a private matter.' So a 'private' matter is the same as a 'secret' matter!"

"Mom," Flora says, "look up 'secret.' "

"Sec . . . Second thought . . . Secret . . . Secret! . . . 'Secret,' " Nanny reads from the dictionary. " 'One, kept from or acting without the knowledge of others. Two, Beyond general understanding; mysterious. Three, concealed from sight; hidden.' "

"Weird," Flora says. " 'Private' can mean 'secret,' but 'secret' doesn't mean 'private.' "

"Jack," Alice says, "is that the revised edition?"

The potato salad vanishes. "Last sausage, anybody?" Jack says.

"I'll split it with somebody," Nanny volunteers.

"Ahem." Jack raises his spoon and taps his glass. "To my beloved wife."

They clink.

"And to her friends. And"—he turns to the girls—"to the dazzling next generation."

They tap glasses twice more.

"Oh!" Betsy says. "You're both wearing the bracelets!"

"Would you like mine?" Alice fidgets the clasp.

"No way. Mom wanted you and Aunt Nanny to have them. She thought they'd make you laugh."

"Your mother was right, darling." Alice decides that when she gets home she will destroy the letter and forget she saw it. "Now," she continues, "I want to hear everything about the Debussy. How is it progressing, Betsy?"

"Well, you know it started with the Web, right?" Betsy talks about researching Debussy, how finding something led to something else that led to something that led to an unfinished violin sonata. "Debussy scored part of it, then put it aside, and now I'm working on scoring the rest of it. I'm channeling Debussy." She laughs. "How's that for hubris?"

Flora shifts in her seat. She says: "Do you miss my dad, Uncle Jack?"

Jack thinks. "What I miss most, Flor, is the six of us." He turns to Nanny and Alice. "I miss the idea of all of us growing old together. In the woods."

"You were part of the Berkshire Plan?" Alice turns to Nanny. "*You* were?"

"My mother *invented* the Berkshire Plan," Alice says.

Everybody carries in dishes. Nanny is about to excuse herself to look at the books when Alice says, "Sit, Jack. Nanny and I insist on cleaning up."

"Want me to help, Mom?" Flora asks.

"Why don't you girls go to the movies?" Nanny suggests.

"I have to go back to the office," Flora says.

"Oh Flor. We haven't done this in years," Betsy says. "I never see you. Please?"

The girls decide on the new Almodóvar and rush out. They wait for the elevator. Laughter burbles from the hallway.

Nanny scrapes plates. Alice files them in the dishwasher. Nanny frets about getting to the books.

Jack uncorks a bottle of pink Moscati and fills three cordial glasses.

"It makes me happy when the girls do things together," he says.

"Me too," Nanny agrees.

Suddenly there is nothing left to do.

"More Moscati?" Jack wags the bottle.

"No thanks," Alice says. "Jack, this was perfect."

His hand drifts along the books as they make their way to the hall closet. "You girls were always borrowing books from each other," he says.

Last chance, Nanny thinks. "Jack, I could use something good to read."

"Help yourself. You too, Alice."

He sits on the center of the couch and sips his drink.

Alice joins Nanny at the shelves. Their friend was meticulous about her books. Fiction by author alphabetically. Religion and mythology on the same shelf. Plays and poetry had theirs. Paris-in-the-twenties all together, even if poetry got mixed with fiction and plays. Art books. Memoir with biography. Science next to child care. Shelves and shelves of psychology.

Alice locates exploration next to travel. She is thrilled to see biographies of Sir Ernest Shackleton and Fabian Gottlieb von Bellingshausen.

Nanny's eyes dance over the spines. They stop on history.

"Pssst," she says.

Alice is flipping through the latest book about Apsley Cherry-Garrard. She closes it and walks over to Nanny.

Nanny points to three titles.

"Do you believe?" she whispers.

"Believe *what*?" Alice whispers back.

In the living room they show their selections to Jack.

"These okay?" Nanny proffers three books.

"Sure." Jack flaps his hand. "Take as long as you want."

He helps them with their coats. Nanny checks the hangers. Bobbie's cape is still there.

"I'll get these back to you," Alice says, waving Lansing's *Endurance* and the Cherry-Garrard.

"No rush," Jack says.

He opens the front door and rings for the elevator. The three of them listen for the grind of the rising cab. They wait. Jack clears his throat. He raises his hands and pats both women on the shoulder. It is a gesture of consolation, the kind that says, "There, there. There, there."

Downstairs, waiting for cabs, Nanny thumps her books.

"Guess what, Alice," she says. "We got a gold mine here."

17 · The Smiling Stewardess

If Betsy and Jack find out, it will not be from me. I slip the letter out of my lingerie bag. In the bathroom I tear it to bits, then flush. *Fini.*

Those Civil War books. What loopy plot is that woman hatching now? I will not be part of it. Roberta's business is no longer mine.

Now. Page one.

Endurance!

Sir Ernest Shackleton. Are there still men of that scale? Today, with space-age fabrics, men cannot duplicate what Sir Ernest did in a deerskin anorak.

Is that a key in the door? This is Wednesday. Wednesday is squash night. What on earth is Charles doing home?

He closes in.

"Hey."

I put my finger on the line I'm reading and look up. "Hey, darling."

He stands there. Once the way I loved him was intense. He gave me something to love. Dearest Willie. You knew.

For everything that's lovely is
But a brief, dreamy, kind delight

I go back to Sir Ernest and hot milk.

"That dinner?" Charles points to the mug.

"I was at Jack's. Remember?" This time I don't look up.

"I was thinking we'd grab something."

"I'm in bed, Charles. And I've eaten."

111

"Keep me company, then?"

"Charles. It's nine-thirty-seven. Do you think that is a reasonable request?"

I decide not to ask why he didn't call if he did not intend to play squash. I would have canceled dinner at Jack's. Charles comes first. But now I am so looking forward to semi-frozen men making their way through tide rips in the treacherous Weddell Sea.

"Guess I'll order in," he says.

"Excellent idea. Would you mind closing the door on your way out? I'd rather not hear the television."

"I thought I'd eat in here."

"No room, dearest." I wave my palm at the magazines and catalogs slathered on his former side of the bed.

Since last Wednesday, Charles has been sleeping in the boys' room. Roberta would call this an intervention. She would have approved. Somebody does something so dramatic, it changes an established pattern. Roberta called interventions "the radical surgery" of marriage-and-family therapy. "Instant results," she said. "Things are either better or worse. But they're not the same."

And now Charles will sleep in the boys' old room and perhaps something good will come of it. Like that elderly couple Roberta treated. Every night for sixty years, the husband screamed at dinner. Finally the wife could not bear it one more night. She went to see Roberta:

"He yells at me. Every night, he finds a reason. I can't take it anymore."

"What do you do when he yells?" Roberta asked.

"I yell back. What would you do?"

"Have you got a metal pot in the kitchen?"

"Who doesn't?"

"And a wooden spoon?"

"Of course."

"Tonight when your husband yells, I want you to walk into the kitchen, get the pot, and start banging it with the spoon. Don't stop till he stops yelling. Just keep banging the pot. Don't tell him why. When he stops yelling, hang up the pot. I want you to do that every night."

The woman returned the following week. "The first night," she told Roberta, "he was so angry. He said, 'What are you doing?'"

"And?"

"I just kept banging the pot like you said, and he screamed, 'What are you, crazy?' but I kept on banging. When he stopped yelling, I stopped banging. The second night when he started yelling I went into the kitchen and got the pot again. This time he said, 'Stop doing that!' but I kept banging till, same as the night before, he shut up. The third night when he started yelling I pushed up from the table and before I got to the pot he went quiet and that was Tuesday and he hasn't yelled since."

The woman asked for another appointment.

"Why?" Roberta asked.

"I need you to tell me how to get a mink."

Would Roberta regard our new sleeping arrangement as an "intervention"? Or is it a "controlling act"? Is settling Charles in the boys' room one of the three most abusive things I've done to him? What could be the other two? Discarding his college beer-bottle collection? We were living in one room. Not allowing his mother to babysit? She wept openly about Charles' father to the boys.

What are the three worst things Charles has done to me? I put *Endurance* down. One comes to mind. How I loathe it: Charles waggling up behind me, always when my hands were occupied, then grabbing my breasts. I told him each time I could not bear it. He would wait until I was carrying plates to the kitchen or diapering one of the boys and he'd spring. He would wait until I was defenseless. He would laugh.

Telling Charles not to do what he enjoyed, was that abusive? Did grabbing please him more than it peeved me?

Perhaps someone handed Charles that brochure on the street

and he stuck it in his pocket. Surely I would know if my husband felt abused.

Charles hangs up his suit. He stretches on his navy sweats.

"Good night, dear," I say. "Please don't forget the door."

Charles closes it behind him, a gesture as definitive as the moment a smiling stewardess pulls the drape between you and First Class.

18 · Bigger than God

Takata-takata.

Takata-tak.

Takata-tak-tak-tak.

Savion Glover is tap-dancing in my bathroom, or the heat is coming up.

I flip through Bobbie's books. George Bemis, author of *The Reddest Night* and *She Said What?*, published by Random House. Haney Jeff Watts, author of *Beauregard and Bobby,* published by Scribner. Dale Rawlinson, Ph.D., author of *The Sunday Leg: A Compleat History of North Carolina Hand-Made Civil War Prosthetics,* published by Duke University Press.

Three books about the Civil War. Nothing in the acknowledgments. None of them inscribed. No dedications to Roberta Heumann Bloom, Bobbie, RHB, or BB.

I could Google all three authors and see if one's also a therapist, but what would that tell me? Did Bobbie meet him at a psych conference? One of those gigonda hotels with simultaneous conventions? Should I e Alice and suggest a meeting with a detective? She wants to help now. Looking at Betsy tonight, how could she not? Her whole life she knows Bobbie. We could call that guy Bobbie's friend Cookie Litt used, the private eye who dressed like a maintenance worker and sifted through her husband's Skadden, Arps trash.

I almost kill myself getting into the shower. The cracks between the white hexagonal floor tiles are uneven. My bathroom floor has fault lines. Buildings never stop settling. If I squint, my floor has varicose veins.

I'm settling too. Drying off, I take inventory. The face-lift test, four fingers horizontal between hairline and brow. They fill the span so I'm not a candidate yet. Since I only smoked in college, I don't have a pleated upper lip. Shoulders never age. But what was the flabby arm-part called? The triceratops? Tripods? Hands okay. Breasts? If not exactly perky, they're still looking up. Stomach? I have Flora to show for it. How do these new mothers spring back into shape? Boing! Two weeks postpartum and they're whizzing through apartments. My thighs. Well I'm not ready for a bathing suit with a skirt yet. My ass? You called it "the Land o' Plenty," Freddy. And you liked it that way. In all, I'm aging better than the bathroom floor.

I pull on my nightie and get a glass of ice water. In the little room, I drop Bobbie's books next to the computer. I stroll through the dining room and turn out the lights. I pass the door to Flora's room. I haven't been in it since—when? All those nights—colds, earaches, thirst, bogeymen, growing pains, bad dreams—she called to me. The heat that rose off that child's body. The girl burned coal. Where did she get that? Freddy didn't give off heat. Unless you count methane.

I climb on top of her bed. Flora's room is the guest room now, dependably neat. No mounds of rejected jeans, nests of thongs. No nail-polish bottle polished to the desk. Where is Flora in this room? The fishbowl of matches from high school. The framed kindergarten collage made of felt scraps Freddy used to say cost $140,000, because that's what private school tuition was by the time you got through. "Nans, we gotta insure the collage," he liked to say. "It's the most valuable thing we've got."

Her old window overlooks Madison Avenue. In her new apartment she overlooks an air shaft. No light, no sky. Flora calls before work to ask me if it's raining. Her old bedroom is bigger than her apartment. Tenements were more humane. Tenements are prime now. The only bad real estate left in New York is my daughter's apartment. Will she ever live as well as she did growing up? She'd have to marry André Heinz.

Her bathroom door is open. There's a full-length mirror on it. The mirror reflects the bottom of my feet poking out below my nightie. Interesting perspective, like that Renaissance portrait of Christ laid out, skin lifeless white. You see him foreshortened from his soles back. Masaccio? Murillo? *Mantegna!* I bring my knees to my chest. I spread my legs. Hmmmm. I'm violet. A grape lollipop. It's been three years, Freddy. I miss you. I miss you on me. On me, under me, over, around, and through. I miss weight. I miss playing Dr. Yes with you and Substitute Teacher. All I had to do was bend over. That you wanted me made me ready.

Am I too old for desire? Did your death neuter me? It's not fair. Men have so many years, decades when their gorgeous, cleaving, hard-curved horns exist purely for pleasure. Soon as a girl hits puberty, she's in service to her parts. She can't say the word, but she's a slave to it. Suddenly it goes from something you never thought about to urgent cosseting and vigilance. Forty years of six days a month doting on it, interrupted only by pregnancies. Painful life-threatening unaesthetic methods of birth control, Pap smears, then laser surgery for bad Pap smears, then . . . what? What's the next insult? Vaginal Alzheimer's? Your cervix excised and plunked in a stainless-steel tray? Why can't it just snap off so you could drop it at the dealers like a Honda. Bring it in for service. "Got some miles on her." The mechanic would wipe his hands with a rag. "But we fixed her up real good. Purring like new. Here ya go, ma'am. Ready to roll."

Bobbie said Linda Bassin hadn't had sex for seven years after her divorce. Then she met a man. Everything worked. Will I ever make love again? Where's that stir?

I stretch my legs out and point my toes. STIR, I think. STIR, STIR, STIR. I point my toes so hard my shins shake. I imagine your hairy heft on me, pressing down, skin to skin, wet to wet.

STIR, STIR, STIR. I imagine you saying, "Let me see you. I want to see how you're made." STIR, damnit. I see you naked introducing yourself at the foot of the bed. "Good morning, class." STIR. "I'm your substitute teacher. Today we will study . . . *reproduction.* Do I have a volunteer?"

STIR, STIR, STIRRRRRRRR.

Stir stirs. I feel it, the blessed involuntary clench. Another. Still works.

In the kitchen I invert my water glass on the old porcelain drain board. Bobbie would tell me to sell this barn. She'd be on my case. She'd hate I worry about money. But if I sold my home, what would I net? What would be left after the flip tax, the fees, capital gains, and the $250,000 New York penalty for living alone? Enough to buy a smaller place plus a down payment on a one-bedroom for Flora? Would I have enough for the Berkshire Plan? Bobbie thought it could work. She'd have made it work. She was Clyde Beatty in the center ring. Is that what Flora didn't like about her? Bobbie could get people to do anything. Like those newlyweds that wouldn't stop fighting.

"All right, you two," she told them. "First I need to know: do you both want to stay in this marriage?"

"Yes!"

"Then you'll do whatever I say?"

"We will!"

"Whenever you fight, whenever you start in, it's Tango Time."

"What's that?" the husband asked.

"Do you know how to tango?"

"No."

"Perfect! Both of you have to get undressed and tango naked to Fred Astaire singing 'I Love a Tango.' "

It never failed.

"When couples fight," she told me, "they can't hear each other. First, you gotta stop the fighting."

"Naked tangos stop fighting?" I asked.

"Here's the CD," Bobbie said. "Get back to me."

Tomorrow's a big day. I've got the Turners at ten-thirty. Their kids are grown so they're moving in from Greenwich. Clearys at three. *Mr.* Cleary. They won't see apartments together. Twice as much work, but they'll have no trouble passing the board. Six o'clock, the Glogowers and the Black Hole of Calcutta. How do you put a baby in a sunless apartment? Poor kids. It's not that they don't have the financials. Inventory stinks.

I check my e. No, I do not have erectile dysfunction. Jeanette wants an update on the Hahn place. Flora forwards what to do if you think you're having a heart attack driving a car. I don't have a car.

For fun, I Google "Civil War." I go to the bottom of the page and hit NEXT about a thousand times. I go back to the first page. Holy moly. 38,100,000 sites for "Civil War"! I refine my search: "American Civil War." 25,300,000! "Civil War" must be the biggest category on the Internet. As big as "God"? I type in "God." God has 62,000,000 sites! Is that good for God? What does "love" have? Is "love" bigger or smaller than "God"? "Love": 178,000,000! Love is bigger than God and the Civil War combined! What about "friend"? I type in "friend." 223,000,000! "Friend" is bigger than "Civil War" and "God" together, but not as big as "God," "Civil War," and "Love."

What's "Secret"?

194,000,000!

What's "Private"?

Results for "Private": 1,800,000,000!

"Private" is bigger than "Civil War," "God," "Love," "Friend," and "Secret" combined.

. . .

None of the book jackets have photos. I read the bios and jot down the authors' names. Should I send a letter care of their publishers? Too risky. What if it got lost in the mailroom or buried on a desk? I check the flaps again. All three mention where the author lives. I Google "White Pages" and get their addresses. How strange not to use the phone book anymore. Flora's children will be wide-eyed she was born when people thumbed numbers up in a ten-pound book.

I open my desk drawer and remove six envelopes. I sign off the Internet and get into Word:

Mr. Haney Jeff Watts
1745 Peachtree Lane
Rome, Georgia 30165

Dear Mr. Watts,
   A letter has come into my possession that may be of interest to you.

Too formal.

Dear Mr. Watts,
   Bobbie (Roberta?) Bloom? Roberta (Bobbie?) Bloom? left a letter you wrote to her to me. (To me and a another friend? Left me a letter as well as to another friend?) Want it back?

Too easy to say no to.

Mr. Watts:
   The late Bobbie Bloom was my best friend. I have a letter you sent her. Would you like it back?

What if he doesn't know she's dead?

Dear Mr. Watts,
    I am trying to find the author of a letter that has come into my possession. The letter was sent (addressed?) to one Bobbie (Roberta?) Bloom. Are you the author? (Might that be you?) If so, the letter's yours for the asking.

Yuk.

Dear Mr. Watts,
    My dear friend Bobbie Bloom asked me to contact you.

Liar, liar, pants on fire.

Dear Mr. Watts,
    Alice Vogel and I were friends of Roberta Bloom. Were you?

That's it. I press PRINT. The Watts letter churns out. I change the names and addresses for Rawlinson and Bemis, then print two more. I stamp SASEs. Should I e one to Alice before I mail them, see what she thinks? It's not like I need her permission. What if no one answers? What if all three write back saying they don't know Bobbie? Where am I then? If I had unfinished business, I'd make it clear what I wanted my friends to do. What's the point of a mystery? Unless she didn't know what to do with the letter herself. Still, to go to the trouble of renting a box when you're dying. Why not do what Jackie O did? Reread and light the fireplace.
    The phone rings.
    "Hello?"
    "Nanny? Janie Achs."
    "Janie. I'm so glad to hear your voice. We didn't get to talk at the funeral."

"Lordy. It's just so raw, honey."

"I still can't believe it. Can you?"

"You know, Nanny? Every time I think about her? I get so flipped I have to blow in a brown paper bag."

"This isn't supposed to happen. Not yet."

"People our age, dropping like flies," Janie says.

"Had you seen her recently?" I probe.

"Honey, after Owen left, I didn't want to see a soul. I even stopped looking in the mirror."

"Sorry about Owen."

"Yes, well. He had it coming. No pun intended."

"I had dinner at Jack's the other night." If Janie knows anything, she'll tell me now.

"What's the story? How's Jack doing? He going through with that Berkshire thing?"

"You were part of that too?"

"Tell the truth, Nanny? Now that Bobbie's gone? In twenty years or so I'm moving to that senior vineyard in California where they let you press grapes."

I lick the envelopes. Oh what's the point. I don't have enough to do? Recent Alarming News About Myself: if I come across a paper clip, I stop what I'm doing, pick up the paper clip and carry it through the apartment till I find the paper-clip holder.

Will I die in this wreck, this hulk with our history sunk in its beams, paper clips everywhere, sagebrush blowing down the hall?

If no one answers, I'll know I've done my best.

Maybe I'll Google H-A-N-E-Y J-E-F-F W-A-T-T-S. Haney Jeff Watts has four pages? No photos on the book jackets. What does he look like?

Here's a panel discussion from a meeting.

A group shot.

WATTS, H. J. Third row, third in. Must be tall. Tall guys stand in the back. Hard to see him. How do you blow things up? A blowup icon should look like a balloon. I press something. Nothing happens. I pound it, though Flora says that doesn't help. Suddenly black blobs fill the screen. The dots that make up the photo are so big, I can't link them into features. Black Blobs could be George Washington.

I get another glass of water. It's dark out. The man across the way is walking naked from his bathroom to his bedroom. He's in the shower cap. My kitchen light is off, he thinks he's safe. No one stands in a dark kitchen watching out the window. Right.

I take the water back to the computer and dial up AOL.

> From: nannypoo@aol.com
> To: Luba1102@earthlink.com
> Subject: help
> Alice—We gotta talk.

19 · Operating on a Presumption

The Bergdorf's model sweeps toward their table.

"Next December, Luba will get seven fifty for that," Alice says. "Some soul's New Year's dream-come-true."

The waistband of the Lurex pantsuit falls five inches below the navel.

"What next?" Nanny blinks. "The pubic ruff? Pubic hair-styling?"

It surprises Alice that Nanny takes an interest in the models. This is the fourth time they have met, and each time Nanny has worn the same black suit. Alice suspects Nanny has several, a uniform of sorts.

"Incidentally," Alice remarks, "I had no idea you'd be at Jack's the other night."

"Same here," Nanny says. "Think they had a good marriage?"

"Nobody knows about someone else's marriage." Alice adjusts the collar of her shirt. "But what do you suppose it was like, being married to someone who commandeered the light?"

"You think Jack was neglected?"

"He was the man who opened the wine, who carried in the birthday cakes and held the door."

"He liked carrying the cake, Alice."

"On balance, I believe it was a working marriage."

"What's a 'working marriage'?"

"One that is still together."

Nanny considers. "Think they ever thought about divorce?"

"Who hasn't?"

"Me," Nanny says. "Not seriously. The man never bought a towel. Fred went straight from his mother to me."

"The other night," Alice steers the conversation, "what were your impressions?"

"I was creeped out having information they didn't have. I hate that."

"You're operating on a presumption," Alice says.

"Huh?"

"You're behaving as if your presumption is true. You don't know they don't know. In any case, I was pleased both of us were there. It made it easier for them, more festive."

"My mother died forty-two years ago, and sometimes I still get sideswiped. And I'm sure Bobbie told you about my husband."

"Horrible."

"Are your parents still alive?"

"My mother."

"Lucky you. There's no one left who's known me my whole life. What kind of shape is she in?"

Alice starts to say "bedridden." Then she envisions her mother underneath her mattress, being ridden by it. "My mother has spinal stenosis," Alice replies. "But her brain is first-rate."

"What a trade-off. Bad body, good brain. Good body, bad brain. Too bad you never get bad body, bad brain. You wouldn't know you were falling apart."

"If life were fair, we'd be bored to tears."

"If life were fair," Nanny says, "the world would be living in low-income housing."

Their Gothams arrive. Alice gets down to business. "You wanted to have lunch?"

"Those books I took at Bobbie's? They all had to do with the Civil War."

"And?"

"Remember how the letter started?"

Alice thinks. " 'Lincoln pondering'?"

"If the guy knew so much about the Civil War, I figured maybe he wrote a book about it. Remember? In the letter? The 'reading my book to you' part?"

"Vaguely."

"I mean, who knows, off the top of their head, about a pivotal night at Fort Sumter?"

"And?"

"I read the bios on the jacket flaps. One's a history professor, one's a lawyer, one's also a novelist."

Alice rakes her salad.

"I don't know how to interpret your silence," Nanny says.

"I tore up my copy of the letter."

"You tore it up?"

"It's gone."

Nanny thinks. "You know, if I had a chance at having a man love me like this guy loved Bobbie, I might grab it."

Alice shifts in her seat. "Loving someone other than my husband is not part of my worldview."

"Even when Fred was alive, I'm not a hundred percent sure I'd've been able to say no to this experience. I mean, despite everything I know about sex. Think about your lovers. Were you ever loved like this?"

Alice considers this a private question. She does not care for women who equate openness with intimacy. She suspects that soon she will have to hear that a used teabag was Nanny's preferred method of birth control. Or that her husband could only perform when he envisioned Clarabelle with a seltzer bottle.

"I'm a bit older than you," Alice says. "I missed the sexual revolution by five minutes."

"I got in under the wire."

"I must tell you," Alice continues. "We seem to have a different way of regarding Roberta's—how to say this?—*disclosure.* I don't give a fig if she had an affair. Or why. Or who it was with. Roberta's private life, her secret life, is of no consequence to me. Nor, frankly, should it be."

"No, Alice. *You* don't get it. I don't give a flying fuck about the affair either. I don't care if she had a lover. I don't care if she swung from a chandelier with Tarzan. Hello? Hello? You listening, Alice? It's that she wanted us to do something. Can we please, please, please agree on that?"

Alice says nothing.

"You want to know what it *is* about?"

"What you *think* it is about," Alice corrects.

"It's about what she wanted. Okay? So let's figure out what to do, because she wanted us to do something. And that'll be the end of it. And by the way, thanks for e-mailing the time frame."

"Did it help?"

"I don't know. Not yet. It might."

"Those books. Were any signed? You might compare the handwriting to the letter. It was distinctive."

"No signatures. Nothing in the acknowledgments. No dedications. I was hoping, but—you know, Alice?—what if Jack opened a book and read, 'To Bobbie, my beloved muse.'"

Alice frowns. "Perhaps the books had nothing to do with the lover. Perhaps Roberta already had them."

"Really?" Nanny asks. "You think every home library has three Civil War books?"

"I have two. The Civil War was our *Iliad*."

"In the meantime, I Googled their addresses and sent each guy a letter," Nanny says.

"What did you say?"

"'Alice Vogel and I were friends of Roberta Bloom. Were you?'"

"That's *all*?"

"What do you mean?"

"That is the letter in its entirety? You didn't mention Roberta had died? That her friends had a letter?"

"Excuse me," Nanny says. "Did I forget this wrong? You wanted editorial input?"

"I would have helped had you asked me."

"Well, that's encouraging," Nanny says. She takes her bag off her lap. She unzips the top. "In that case, I made a list of possible motives." She unfolds a piece of paper and begins to read. "*Uno*, part of me thinks it's what we talked about when we went to the vault. That she wanted us to know she was happy. But then I think—two—why, if the Share Her Happiness Theory is right, did she wait till after she died? Which brings me to three: Did he know she got cancer? And if not, were we supposed to tell him? In other words, number four: When did it end? Does he know Bobbie died?"

"Nothing in the letter says it ended. We only know it ended because Roberta's dead."

"But we know about Thursday, August 1, 2002. And thanks to you, we know she was away the fourth, fifth, and sixth." Nanny thinks. "Remember when she began to leave town? There were meetings. We had to earn credits to keep our licenses up. Suddenly she was going to all of them. The Impossible to Reach Bobbie Era. How odd," Nanny considers, "to think she lied to me."

"This is so Roberta," Alice says.

"What do you mean?"

"She was mischievous."

"Be specific."

"Are you on the mailing list for any sex-aid catalogs?"

"That's Bobbie?"

"Here's my favorite: Roberta and I had prepaid for a week at a fabulous spa. We were sharing a room. The very first night, I bumped into the metal bed frame. I was certain I'd sheared off my ankle bone. The pain was shocking. I lay on the bed and asked Roberta to tell me precisely how bad it was, not to spare me anything. I felt the heat of blood, the chill of bone exposed to air. I was too terrified to look. I was positive blood was spurting and the ankle was splintered and I was going to spend the rest of my pre-paid spa week in bed."

"And?"

"Roberta looked at it and shrieked, 'Oh my God! This is the worst thing I've ever seen! You're going to need surgery! I better call the front desk! Maybe the spa has a doctor!' And I kept saying, 'Oh no! Oh no!' and 'Call an ambulance!' and then Roberta started laughing, and I said, 'Why are you laughing?' and she said, 'Look at it!' and I didn't want to but she insisted, so eventually I did, and all it was was a little pink. It hadn't broken the skin."

"But I loved that about Bobbie. She was playful. She made me laugh at myself."

"You must remember," Alice says, "we were two girls without sisters thrust together much of our childhood. There was games-manship. She was an expert."

Nanny is struck by the words. Flora and Betsy were thrust together too. She understands there is much that went on between them she cannot know. "So you think the letter is some kind of game?"

"What I'm saying is, I knew Roberta a way you did not. Leaving us a letter with no instructions, that would be in character."

"But you loved her, Alice."

"She was my dearest friend."

"So let's see this through. I want to find this guy. I'm in till the end, whatever that is. Dying people don't play tricks."

Alice nods for the check. "It would be lovely to divine what she wanted, Nanny. But that is not possible. And although I'd like to help you, in the end I must vote for forgetting we saw the letter. There is too much of an opportunity to hurt people. Three days in August she couldn't be reached? Three Civil War books?" Alice shakes her head. "There's an awful lot at stake."

"You don't want to find him?"

"If it were me—my love letter left behind?—that would not be my wish. Would it be yours? Think about it, Nanny."

"Number five on my list is: She wrote to him too and she wanted us to retrieve *her* letter. A simultaneous swap."

Alice thinks. "So Betsy and Jack would never, under any circumstances, see it? Why not ask him for it?"

"See?" Nanny says. "You do want to know."

"Let's say you do find him. Then what?"

"Do I have to figure that out now?"

"No. I don't see how you could."

"How many times in your life do you get to wing it like this? To have no idea how it'll wind up?" Nanny says.

When your children move away, Alice thinks. When your mother dies. When the police call to say your husband has fallen down in the street or gotten run over by a truck or run someone else over. When you sleep with someone not your husband. "I suppose that's what defines an adventure," Alice says.

"What?"

"Not having any idea how it will turn out."

20 · Perfect Extra-Large

In the end, there are two choices: Try to agree on what we would have wanted done. Or try to intuit what Roberta wanted.

What good could possibly come of this?

I must not get roped in further.

"Lovely," I say. Yumi is vacuuming the ceiling. She is the first intern to do so. One gets blind to stalactites of dust, to what one wishes were not there. Luba has never looked so crisp. That child climbed a ladder to do it.

Ironic. Yumi knows clothes. Yet clothes will never look good on her. Yumi's body is compressed. She is built what Mother calls "low to the ground." No matter how she holds her head, Yumi can never be elegant. What Yumi has in excess is energy. Energy redeems. It can make a woman beautiful.

And Yumi has style. Not my style, but style nonetheless. One might call her look the Prerogative of Youth. Jeans under skirts. Sweaters on backward. Two pullovers, different lengths. Long-sleeved *under* short. Jewel-neck under vee. Exposed to the finest clothes in the world, what has Yumi absorbed? Socks rippled like stacks of flapjacks. On top of fishnets. Those "combos" she designs.

Every year, Luba accepts an intern from FIT. Some are better than others. Yumi, although she does not dress like Luba's clientele, is easily the best. She maintains the shop with exquisite, uncomplaining care. She is unfailingly Old World gracious to the customers. She takes joy in her work and has the two things essential for it: Yumi loves to shop, which means she knows everything out there and what it costs. And she has an eye. Beyond that, Yumi

131

can sew. She makes delicate repairs when necessary and I'd rather hand her the twenty than a dressmaker. Once Yumi replaced the black buttons on a de la Renta suit we were going to dispose of. She fashioned the buttons out of plastic sushi one sees in windows of Japanese restaurants. The suit had languished. It sold that day.

"What do you think, Alice?"

Yumi has taken out a summery Pucci pantsuit. There are not many designers one gets tired of twice in a lifetime.

"Yumi? This? For your first window?"

"It's aspirational, Alice. It will remind people to make reservations for St. Bart's."

"But it's a pantsuit, Yumi. Luba has no legs."

"No problem, Alice. Put the jacket on Luba, fling the pants on the back of a chair. Have a toppled champagne glass and lace panties on the floor. A mise-en-scène, Alice. We tell a story with clothes."

"It's your window, Yumi. But first, bags." I point to the mountain of unretrieved clothes spilling out of the wayback. After ninety days, if consigners fail to pick them up, we bag unsold clothes and donate them.

"You should be able to fit them in five Hefty bags, Yumi. Could you call—let's see—who picks up the same day?"

"Arthritis Thrift Shop."

"Yes. Good. Arthritis. Call them and tell them they must take the bags this afternoon."

"Can I have them, Alice?"

"You want these?"

"Just this, this, and this. And this. Oh and this and this." She grabs an evening gown, two dresses, a sequined jumpsuit, an armload of sweaters, a pleated skirt.

"More combos, Yumi?"

"You got it, Alice. Take the right sleeve off. Slit the back." Yumi uses her free hand to mime disembowelment. "Close it with a diaper pin. New pockets, new collar. Deconstruct! Make old clothes brand-new!"

"They're yours," I say. But since it is my responsibility to educate the intern, I add, "And who will buy these combos, Yumi? You must consider your target audience."

Yumi puts her hands on her hips. "Alice, when was the last time you were downtown?"

"I had lunch at Bergdorf's yesterday."

"Alice, that's not downtown. That's uptown."

"No, Yumi. We are uptown. If Bergdorf's is uptown, what is Eighty-third Street?"

"Eighty-third and Madison? We're in the burbs here, Alice. Eighty-third is the country."

"Take whatever you want, Yumi."

"Will you let me put a combo in the window, Alice?"

"Yumi, would Mrs. Vandervoort wear a combo?"

"Alice, you want young customers in Luba or dying customers?"

I can't believe this child calls me Alice. Yumi borders on rude. "I tell you what, Yumi, when you're ready to do a window, I will give you free rein. But if no one shows interest in, say, three days, we will change it. Does that sound fair?"

"Alice, you got a deal."

Yumi squirrels her finds in the wayback. That is where we store the bags, do the books, keep the hot plate and tea service, along with a tiny fridge and Jason's old aluminum baseball bat, Luba's in-house security. A bat is essential for a ground-floor boutique.

The bell has not rung today. Yumi and I hang Christmas twinkle lights in the window. It's fifty-eight degrees outside. We fling Ivory Flakes on Luba's shoulders. When New York gets a lovely day in December, it is too nice to be indoors shopping. When December turns nasty, who wants to go out and shop? I check my date book. I could drop by Mother's, then pick up crab cakes at Fairway. Charles loves them with rémoulade. What could possibly be the three worst things I've done? Surely the bed. But he had that brochure prior to the first night he spent in Jason's bed. Was it my reluctance to lend his father more money, even though we did? The summer I began distance-swimming and Charles had to entertain the boys? What would Roberta think of confronting one's partner with a list of abuses? Has Charles noticed his hair is missing?

I'd best stick around. There's much to do. When Yumi emerges from the back, I say, "All right. We've put it off long enough. Let's do Nadine."

Nadine Flato drives in from Long Island to drop her things off. She is a solid 18, a perfect extra-large, who squeezes into a 14.

We unzip the bags. Yumi hauls out a black jacket.

"Ay!" She winces. "Look at this, Alice."

"It looks all right to me, Yumi."

"Look in the light, Alice. The lapel. She covered egg yolk with black Magic Marker."

Sure enough, there's a shiny purple-black crust.

Yumi shrieks at the silk lining of an armpit. It has shredded. "Ew! What's she take us for? Junk shop?"

White perspiration rings, split seams, derailed zippers, ambushed stains. Grand-mère was right. Heavy people are harder on clothes. All that rubbing. They wear them out from the inside.

"Nadine's a new low, Alice." Yumi shakes her head.

But there are also two never-worn pantsuits from Armani, tags still on.

"Hang these on the keeper rack, Yumi. Some perfect extra-large will swoon."

Yumi checks the pants. She shakes her head. "Alice, are you crazy? There's dirt in the cuffs! These are old!"

"These are brand-new, Yumi. See, dear? Tags."

"Yeah, right. Like she doesn't wear them and put the tags back. Like we never see that—right, Alice? Oldest trick in the book. You want me to find the original tag holes?"

Yumi rips the pants off the clip hanger and pulls a leg inside out. She braves the Flato crotch. "Look, Alice. That's new? You tell me."

It has a stain the shape of Florida.

"Pack it all up, Yumi. I don't have the stomach for Nadine. Just, please, pack it up now! If we're lucky, she'll never come back."

"Alice! Not so fast! We got a nice pearl toursade. Sells for five fifty at Barney's."

"That is pretty." I relent, acknowledging the charge of a find. Nadine has at least one necklace in each bag she drops off. Perhaps she forgets she has overripe chins. The main chin, the bottommost, rests on her chest and puffs out like a gecko's. Perhaps when she sees a pretty necklace Nadine forgets it won't be visible.

"We'll get two hundred easy, Alice. And look."

Cupped in Yumi's palms are two Miriam Haskell clip-ons, nests of pink crystal. "These are genuine faux," Yumi says, awed.

She whips out an Hermès scarf. She ties it around her neck the French way then vamps to the front door. On the way, she plucks a pair of Lagerfeld sunglasses from the vitrine then vamps back to me. She could be on a runway. The girl is—what? She's a word you don't hear anymore. Sassy. Sassiness has disappeared. Sassy has reached the realm of normal behavior. There's no need for the word.

We come across five pairs of immaculate Constanco Bastos. What makes a 210-pound size 18 believe she can wear shoes with toe boxes like needle-nose pliers? Two hundred ten pounds of quivering flesh perched on two crushed toes.

Yumi bundles Nadine's rejects to the wayback. We're up to speed.

"Let's do Plesser," I say. "We've earned a treat."

We look forward to Evelyn Plesser. She goes to Syms and Daffy's and buys beautiful things at deep discount. She removes the price tags and brings her finds to me. A Calvin Klein suit currently in Bloomingdale's for $850 is purchased at Loehmann's for

$149 and resold at Luba for five hundred. She gets half and nets a hundred. Clever girl.

It starts to rain. "Yumi, let's put the pink Burberry on Luba."

Yumi hangs the last Plesser on the keeper rack. "Why do people want to see a raincoat when it's raining, Alice? That's gonna cheer them up? Oh," she says. "I forgot to tell you. Larry called. He needs to see you right away."

"Larry?"

"The accountant."

Mr. Fleischman? His first name is Larry?

"He left you this letter, Alice. ASAP, he said."

Yumi hands me a folded piece of paper. She starts to work on the window. I put up tea and read:

Alice—

Luba has been in the red six months running now. We need to talk about refinancing your loan. You can't avoid this any longer. Please call me so we can set up a time.

Sincerely,
Mr. Fleischman

21 · New Rule

All of us face the same direction, same distance apart. Staring straight ahead like a school of fish, we watch a white wall. If we turned the chairs around, we'd be looking through a giant window over jazzy Harlem rooftops. A five-mile vista of architectural syncopation clear to the Empire State Building.

Instead we watch the wall.

The LED sign is on the wall.

"NOW SERVING 44," it reports in orange dots. The ticket I hold says 107.

A man in a brown uniform sits behind a desk. A woman wants to sit too. He'd like her to stand behind a line until her name is called.

"Why I got to stand and they all sitting?" she asks. "I can sit if I want to. You can't make me stand."

"You have an appointment," he says. "You're supposed to wait behind the line. You see that line, lady?"

"I can sit if I want to. I'm tired. I need a chair. I don't get to sit on my sorry ass all day like you do."

Tempers are short at the Social Security office on 125th Street.

Four tellers perch behind bulletproof glass. First you wait in line to see the man in the brown uniform. If you pass muster, you wait in line to see Teller Number 4. Teller Number 4 decides if you qualify to see Teller 1, 2, or 3. Teller 1, 2, or 3 tells you if you're eligible to get called into the back.

I count 114 people. Several have fallen asleep. A couple of coughs don't sound good. Some women brought the grandchildren. One miserable man sits in a wheelchair, both legs straight out in casts. Somebody's got a coconut cake. She's eating it

137

out of the box with a white plastic spoon. This is the only person who looks happy.

We're in for the long haul. Everybody knows the routine. Most have headphones. Five are dressed like Malcolm X. When I get out of here, I'm going straight downstairs to the bakery and reward myself with a coconut cake.

A half-hour drags by. A woman sticks her head out the door. "Wunderlich?"

Eyes break from the wall to check who got lucky.

"I'm Rochelle Swink." The woman smiles. "Follow me, please."

A door locks behind us. We're in a room filled with computers. It looks like the metro desk at a big city paper. Ms. Swink parks herself and asks for my Social Security Number. She types it in.

"I'd like all the benefits I can get as soon as I can get them," I say.

She clacks keys.

"You earned, um, oh my, a little bit less than twenty thousand dollars last year," she says. "Do you, um, think you'll be making that, um, amount when you turn sixty-two?"

"More, I hope. But that's three years from now. How would I know?"

Ms. Swink studies her screen. "The good news is, you have more than enough work credits to be fully vested."

"I'm not surprised. I've been paying Social Security thirty-six years straight."

"Yes, I see." Ms. Swink leans in. Blue light bounces off her face. "But you know"—she studies her computer screen—"the more you make, the less you get."

"I used to make a lot more than twenty."

"I see that," Ms. Swink says.

"And I'm hoping to do better. Eventually."

Ms. Swink tells me that in three years, when I'm sixty-two, at my current earnings rate, I'll get $1,176 a month.

"Why so little?"

"Making twenty thousand, you get less," she says. "Plenty of people at sixty-two don't come close to twenty. That's four hundred a week, Mrs. Wunderlich. That's eighty dollars a day. That's ten dollars an hour. That's above minimum wage."

"So okay, say I'm sixty-two and I'm making twenty thousand a year and the government is giving me eleven hundred seventy-six dollars a month, that's . . . what's that times twelve?"

"Fourteen thousand one hundred twelve." Ms. Swink's been here before. "Plus your twenty. Of course, that's before taxes."

"Wait a minute. I pay taxes on the money I paid into Social Security?"

"New rule."

"What if my building maintenance goes up, Ms. Swink? Or there's an assessment? I'm supposed to live on thirty-four thousand one hundred twelve dollars a year?"

"Lots of people sixty-two live on way less, ma'am. You're living on less yourself now."

"I don't live on that alone. I dip into my husband's pension. Wait. I got an idea. Can you look up how much I've paid into my Social Security?"

Ms. Swink studies her screen. "Sixty-seven thousand, six hundred and fifty-one dollars."

"I could use a hunk of that. That would mean a lot to me. Can I tap that? Is there a penalty?"

Ms. Swink looks at me with sympathy. "You can't, so there isn't."

"What if I wait until I'm sixty-five to get my Social Security? How much would I get then?"

"You can't get it all until you're sixty-six."

"Why?"

"New rule."

"Okay, so how much will I get when I'm sixty-six?"

She types, waits, types again, then studies the screen. "Well, you'd be getting fifteen hundred sixty a month, but you could keep it all, every penny, no matter how much you made, if you can wait till then. You're fifty-nine now? Can you wait seven years?"

"How do I know the rule won't change to seventy?"

"You don't. But if you can wait till you're seventy, you'll get two thousand fifty-nine a month."

"Help me out here, Ms. Swink. I'm a widow. Can I get my husband's Social Security?"

I give her Fred's Social Security Number.

"Let's see. Your contributions were greater than his. And if he were alive, he'd be fifty-nine too. So . . . I'm afraid you'd just get yours."

"Okay. What if I make nothing next year?"

"Since you have your credits, that won't affect what you get when you're sixty-two. But if you take it at sixty-two, we can't start you till three months after your birthday."

"New rule?"

"New rule."

I say the stupidest words in the universe: "Ms. Swink, what would you do if you were me?"

"We're not allowed to give financial advice," she says. "I'm sorry."

"I don't get it. I've had money taken out for Social Security for thirty-six consecutive years. Why can't I get it back?"

"Why does everybody think Social Security belongs to them?" Ms. Swink says. "Ma'am, that is not your money. No way. Uh-uh."

"So whose money is it? Who earned the money? Who earned the interest on it for thirty-six years?"

"That money belongs to Social Security."

"I want it back."

"I know you do, Mrs. Wunderlich. And I want peace in the Middle East."

22 · Loveya

There is a message on the answering machine. It is from Jason.
The obstetrician has told Camille the baby's head is down. She is
two centimeters dilated. Jason was three weeks late. First babies
often are. Still, it is beginning. A miracle on its way.

What Roberta wanted. How can Nanny be certain that is know-
able? Blind faith? Naïveté? Tenacious woman. A good person to
have on your side. Perhaps she is right. Something will make itself
clear. I wonder what her husband was like. The daughter, so offhand about her beauty. It is easy to see Nanny in Flora. Oh if I
could get my hands on that woman. I'd sleek her up. She would
look marvelous in Jil Sander, hair off that face. Her eyes are stellar.

I take my tea into the bedroom. There is much to be thankful
for. My boys survived childhood. A grandchild on the way. Mother
is alive. I have a husband who comes home every night. I must tell
Charles how fortunate we are. Does he realize how fortunate we
are? Surely it is a tribute to my marriage that it is impossible to
conjure significant wounds. Yes, on occasion I returned gifts he
gave me. Was I supposed to let a crimson peignoir decay in my
closet when I could exchange it for Fiorentina pumps? Is it that I
don't say "Loveya" back? I am perfectly content hearing "Loveya"
when he's finished. I'd prefer "I love you." "I love you, *Alice*,"
would be nice. Yet how much it means to hear "Loveya." When the
hospital called to say Father had died, Charles rose out of his chair
and ran his finger down the side of my face. I shall not forget that.
Knowing what someone is capable of, a word, a gesture, even if it
is not the word or gesture you want, means the world.

.   .   .

I prop three pillows behind my head and feel the predictable rip-
ple of pleasure. I adore being in bed this time of year, when the
building heat first comes up. I adore being under Grand-mère's
Austrian wool blanket with rolled velvet trim, listening to wind
chatter the windows.

Did Jack see Roberta as a controlling partner? She certainly ran
that show. Still, Jack did not appear to object. He seemed, in a
word, amused.

I pull the blanket under my chin and prop the book against my
knees. Vilhjalmur Stefansson frostbitten in the Canadian Arctic. I
glance at the clock. Five past six. I cannot, will not, go to sleep
before ten. Absolutely not before nine-thirty. No. I will not. What
next? Bed jackets and hot-water bottles? What exactly are what
people call the indignities of age? If youth is wasted on the young,
what is wasted on a certain age? What does "a certain age" mean?
That we are certain? That experience renders us doubt-free? Do
men reach a certain age?

I turn to the gray middle pages where the photographs are.
Nesting in plump pillows as Sherpas freeze rescuing vainglorious
tourists, tucked in a smooth, soft bed while cannibalism erupts on
the Oregon Trail, my husband en route to me, is a most particular
thrill. You could stitch together a life of particular thrills, piece it
like a quilt.

I don't realize I've fallen asleep until I hear the front door close.
He hangs up his coat, stops at the mail table. He's coming toward
our door. I close my eyes. He's in the room. I feel him next to the
bed. He leans over. He removes the tray. This act of tenderness is
more than I can bear. I flutter my lids.

"Oh." He grins. "She's up."

"I fell asleep, dear."

"How are you, Alice?"

"I'm good, Charles."

"Aren't you going to ask me how squash was?"

"How was squash?"

"I won."

"I'm happy to hear that."

"Thought I'd sleep in here tonight, Alice."

"Oh, Charles. No. I don't think so."

"Why not, Alice? It's my bed too."

"Well I think you know why, Charles. Please don't make me say it."

"It's been a week, Alice. I haven't had a drink."

I swing my legs off the bed. "Well, if it's that important to you to sleep in our bed, Charles, I'll sleep in the boys' room and you can."

Charles steps back. "You'd give up your bed for me?"

"Of course I would, dear."

"Oh Alice," he says, "I could never take your bed. How could I take your bed away from you? I'd never do that. You're my girl."

"All right then, Charles. If you truly wish to sleep in our bed, to sleep in it with me, you may. Under one condition."

"What's that?"

"There is something I would very much like to know."

"I have no secrets, Alice."

"You promise you'll answer me truthfully?"

"When haven't I?"

"All right then, Charles. What I'd like to know is, what are the worst things I've done? In our marriage. To you, that is."

"You want me to tell you?"

"Yes, Charles. I do."

"If I tell you, Alice, I'm afraid I'll hurt you."

"I need to know, Charles."

"I'll hurt you. And you'll be angry with me."

"Please, Charles. You have my word. I won't be angry."

He sits on the edge of the bed. He takes my hand. He turns it over. He presses my palm against his heart.

"You give me your word?"

"I'll only be angry if you don't tell me."

His mouth contorts. His struggle breaks my heart. He squeezes my hand. He looks away. "You don't make me feel welcome," he says.

I wait for the next item. Charles says nothing. His heart pounds under my hand. "All right, Charles. I don't make you feel welcome. Next?"

"That's it, Alice. You don't make me feel welcome. You never have. Not in our bed. Not in our home. Not in our marriage. Not bringing up the boys. Never."

"How do I not make you feel welcome, Charles? I don't know how you can say that."

"I can say it because it's true. It's how you make me feel."

"Am I responsible for how you feel, Charles?"

"Very much so, Alice. Am I at all responsible for how you feel?"

Alice thinks. She picks her words with care. "Were I to think you were unhappy, Charles, I believe I would be utterly miserable."

"You mean that, Alice?"

"Oh, darling. Of course I do."

"Say that again."

" 'Oh, darling. Of course I do'?"

"Again. The first part."

" 'Oh, darling'?"

"That's it, Alice," he says, pulling off his shoes. "Keep saying it. Say it till I tell you to stop."

The first snow. Or is it rain? I check the street lights. Yup, it's snow all right. Swirling up, shorting gravity, nature's bling. People used to say New York snow was equal to its weight in pollution. But New York doesn't burn coal anymore. I stick out my tongue. Fresh, minerally, what sky tastes like.

"Know the first thing Eskimos teach their children?" Freddy asked Flora every first snow.

"What, Daddy?" she'd say, knowing the answer.

" 'Don't eat the yellow snow.' "

The first snow. How can something expected feel like magic?

It's coming down. I make out the Glogowers slogging toward me. They're holding hands. Steven's lips are pressed together. Meredith is wiping her eyes with her sleeve. I can't do my How Happy I Am to See You look.

"What's the matter?"

"Meredith's blood pressure. It's through the roof. She's got to have complete bed rest."

"Oh, Meredith. That's terrible."

"This is it," Steven says. "The last apartment we can see till the baby."

"You've tried so hard." Meredith's voice trembles. "You've been so kind to us, Nanny."

"Now look, guys. I know it's easy for me to say, but I don't want you to worry, okay? Steven? Meredith? I mean it. Maybe we'll get lucky today. And if not, we'll find you something after the baby. That's a promise. I give you my word. Things will open up by then. You'll see. It'll be a whole new market."

We ride the elevator up to Fifth Avenue Classic 6.

The Glogowers are desperate. Desperate enough? This apartment is about compromise. Dark, airless, viewless. On the other hand, the park is across the street, the maintenance is low, it's prewar. The Glogowers like picture moldings and quirky pedestal sinks. They won't have to shell out for somebody else's renovation.

The co-broker opens the door. Gabriella Sinclair-Gault has turned on every light. The place looks like Broadway.

"Nice to see you, Nanny." She nods deeply, like a prelude to a curtsy.

I introduce the Glogowers. Gabriella laughs merrily at nothing. She has just the right character flaws to make it in this business.

"Would you care for a bite?" On the coffee table in the living room she has laid out deli sandwiches cut into spokes. They radiate on a doily. The Glogowers shake their heads. They decline the Perrier and mini-éclairs too.

I scoop up two turkeys and a roast beef. "Don't mind if I do." Enough finger sandwiches, you've got dinner.

Gabriella launches into overdrive. "As you can see, this lovely prewar classic six on Fifth has two windows in the living room."

Yes. The Glogowers can see.

"The floors are original. Oak herringbone in the public rooms, not parquet."

We look at the herringbone. Gabriella's got on her black velvet broker-flats, the ones with frogs sipping martinis.

"As you can see," she continues, "this apartment is practically one of a kind." She holds her arms straight out at her sides with this-could-all-be-yours munificence. "Every doorknob, every hinge, is original hardware."

Steven walks to a living-room window. If he opens it, he'll be able to touch the fire escape across the way.

"Care to see the kitchen?" Gabriella drags him away. "It has the original porcelain drain board!"

Steven tosses me a look. The Glogowers prefer wandering. When I show them a place, I stand by the front door and wait until they're finished. They know how to look at apartments. Counting today, they've traipsed through twenty-nine. Not that they're out to waste my time. The Glogowers are serious buyers. But they know the market is unstable. Not that brokers acknowledge that. We say the market's terrific regardless. We use words like "pent-up demand" no matter how unpent demand is. We throw in "remarkable surge" and "burgeoning economy." We mention "Federal Reserve," "sustained growth," and "upticks." We lace our conversation with "robust," "equity," and "outpace." We never forget the seventies. The real-estate market crashed because brokers said it was crashing. Once they admitted it was crashing, it crashed. Who could blame the Glogowers for looking at twenty-nine apartments? Eventually, they'll talk themselves into a cavelike six or junior four in a white brick postwar with an OPW view and a lobby with gum-pocked industrial wall-to-wall. The Glogower scion will attend private school and fine camps where relationships will cement for networking possibilities later in life. The Glogowers will always be . . . naked? Stripped? *Strapped.* Lives dictated by New York real estate. What price, price?

Gabriella's on them like a lamprey. She tails them into the master bedroom. "Investor's dream!" she squeals. I tuck two more turkey sandwiches in a napkin. "Original everything!" "History beckons!"

Downstairs I ask the Glogowers to please call me when the baby comes. "And meanwhile, know I'm going to keep looking. I'm on your case. We're going to find you exactly what you want."

"Really?" Tears wale Meredith's cheeks.

Steven puts his arm around her shoulders. "That's nice, Nanny," he says. "What makes you think it exists?"

24 · Everything Changes Everything

The ladies' lounge has shrunk again. The construction next door is for a restaurant and Bergdorf's wants it bigger. Another hundred square feet of the ladies' lounge has been sacrificed. With this renovation, the window has vanished. Nanny applies Boca Baby lip gloss in the mirror and blows her bangs. All the pretty potted orchids in the world can't make up for artificial light. Nanny decides she could no longer live in the ladies' lounge at Bergdorf's.

Downstairs, Michael shows her to a banquette.

"Sorry I'm late." Alice rushes in. "A bowling bag was under a seat on the bus. The bomb people came."

"Was it a bomb?"

"Thirteen cinnamon-raisin bagels." Alice catches her breath. She flips the gold alligator on her bag and removes a hankie. "How I hate this. I used to run for an hour without looking like a damp beet."

"Hormones. What was that thing Bobbie used to say?"

" 'A woman's body is like a fish tank. Throw one chemical off, the whole thing goes haywire.' "

"Right," Nanny says.

They order their Gothams.

"I've got my mammogram at three o'clock," Alice blurts.

"Want some wine?"

"Then I'll never cool down."

"There should be restaurants for women over fifty. The air conditioner is turned to 'Cryonic.' "

Alice fans herself with her napkin. "Roberta and I always did our mammos together," she says.

"Who'd she go to?"

"Skinner," Alice says.

"Oh, right. Bobbie called his breast exam the physical equivalent of mumbling." Again Nanny is struck by all the Bobbie-Alice rituals. "We did the gyno. So who do you go with now?"

"Myself. My first mammogram without Roberta."

"Oh."

Alice takes a sip of water. She puts the glass down with delicacy, as if there were a right way and a wrong way to put down a glass.

Nanny gets an idea. "No one should go to a mammo alone," she says. "Want me to go with you?"

"I wouldn't dream of asking you."

"You haven't."

Alice perks up. "Are you sure?"

"No biggie. I don't have to show an apartment till five."

"Well thank you," Alice says. "Thank you more than I can say. It helps to know someone is in the waiting room."

Nanny hears this and realizes there is something she has wanted to know. "Were you with her the day they found it?"

"Yes."

"And? When they find something? What's it like?"

"She didn't tell you?"

Nanny shakes her head.

"It was harrowing. Roberta was in there forever. I had no idea what was happening. Finally a technician came out and said I could go back. There she was, newly tiny . . ."

"Oh no."

". . . hunched in that . . . that *pen* where they keep stale coffee and the video machine. *Pretty Woman* was on."

"Who chooses those things?" Nanny interrupts. "Makes me nuts. Can you think of a worse movie for the mammo limbo room?"

Alice considers. *"One True Thing. Wild Strawberries. Imitation of Life."*

"Then?"

"It unfolded in slow motion. The technicians surrounded us. Dr. Skinner phoned a breast surgeon in the building. They squeezed her in. Everyone was soothing but of course you're utterly paralyzed, and Roberta, who fielded bad news the way people wish they could, Roberta was . . . catatonic. It does not help one iota to know that for women our age, the biggest threat is heart attack."

Nanny's hand stops mid-air. She drops a foiled butter pat back in the bread basket.

"And everyone was relentlessly optimistic. *Cheery.* They said things like . . ." Alice pauses. *What if it's my turn?* she thinks. *What if today I'm the one hearing those words?*

"Like?" Nanny encourages.

"Like, 'We're just being thorough.' And 'We're practicing good conservative medicine.' I helped her get dressed. We took the elevator upstairs and we waited and waited. She did not want to talk so we sat there holding hands." Alice stops. "Is this too detailed?"

"No."

"And of course the waiting room was filled with every phase of misery, the young Hasidic couple with a baby, the old woman with yellow skin and boney hands, mothers with daughters, lost-looking husbands pumping their legs. After an hour they called her name. The films had been sent up. She walked into the back. The surgeon examined her. She dressed, then came out to the waiting room and got me."

Nanny appreciates the neutral way Alice is telling it, blow by blow, no self-aggrandizement of her role.

Recounting that day, reliving it, telling it slowly, reminds Alice of the way women tell the stories of their children's births. Dramatic, highly detailed, no matter how much time has passed.

Decades later, a woman retelling the story of her child's birth, the event is as vivid as if it happened that morning.

She continues: "Then we sat with the doctor and talked to him together, and he said, 'I want you to know that ninety percent of these are nothing.' And I felt such relief, Nanny. And then he said it was good he could not palpate it, that it was very small on the pictures, that those were both encouraging signs. 'Most likely it's a benign cyst,' he said, but he would have to take it out in the next month or so to get the pathology report. He said it casually. But, he said—and I remember these words, Nanny, because they struck me as strange and yet they were comforting—he said in a rather offhand way, 'I'm really not terribly *impressed.*' Such an odd word, isn't it? As if one wanted to impress a doctor with a tumor the size of a plum. The surgeon was sanguine. The episode appeared to be merely another routine rotten thing, a minor medical inconvenience.

"And how happy I was with the ninety percent," Alice continues. "A ninety is an A. Roberta got an A in potential benignness! I clung to that ninety percent as if it were a life raft. But not Roberta. No. She said, 'If the Gestapo lined ten people up against a barn and said, "We're only going to shoot one of you," how would you feel?' "

"But her family had no history."

"Eighty percent don't."

"We're all sitting ducks. Know how I think of my breasts now? Time bombs strapped to my rib cage."

"Precisely."

"Where did they go wrong, Alice? We take these . . . these . . . *things* through life with us. First we can't wait to get them. Then we're humiliated they show. Then we begin to understand their beauty, their wild power. They go from objects of pleasure to mounds of anxiety. They keep changing. Know what my biggest fear is?"

"What?"

"I'm getting my mammo. My breast is pancaked between the glass. The lady goes in the back to press the X-ray button, and she's saying, 'Just one moment, I'm sorry, I'm sorry, you're not wearing deodorant, are you? . . .'"

"Oh Nanny."

" 'I'm sorry, just one more moment, I'm sorry, hold your breath, one more moment, I'm sorry,' and on and on the way they do, then—BOOM!—she gets a heart attack and I'm trapped in the machine and I have to chew my breast off to get out."

"Nanny."

"First my mother. Then my father. Then my husband. Then my friend," Nanny says. "Death changes everything."

"Everything changes everything."

Nanny is taken by surprise. What Alice says strikes her as true. Lately even small events seem loaded with significance. Flora holding the cab door. Getting involved with the Glogowers the way brokers are warned not to. The OPW man.

"Was it just the two of you that day?" Nanny asks. "Did she call Jack?"

"No."

"But he's a doctor. He could have expedited things."

"I asked her if she wanted me to call him."

"Think it had something to do with having a lover?"

"How?" Alice asks. "In what way?"

"That she felt too guilty to call Jack when she needed him. That she wanted the lover with her, not Jack."

"I remember thinking at the time it was protective," Alice says. "I remember thinking: *She doesn't want to worry Jack unless she has to.* But you can't know."

"Right. 'You can't know.' I'll put that in my 'Can't Know' file along with 'Did Cavemen Appreciate Beauty' and 'What Would Beethoven Have Thought of Gershwin.' "

The waitress brings their Gothams.

"Any news from the authors?" Alice asks.

"No. That's why I wanted to have lunch. It's been two weeks since I mailed the letters. If we don't hear anything by, say, New Year's, what should we do?"

"Flush your copy," Alice says. "Like I did."

"Would you consider meeting with a detective?"

"No."

"It's a piece of cake for a private eye."

"Still no."

"Think what you'd want," Nanny says.

"That's the point," Alice says. "I have."

They decide to split a strawberry tart.

"So," Nanny says, "Bobbie talked to you about the Berkshire Plan?"

"Innisfree? Yes."

"Why 'Innisfree'? It had a name?"

"That's where Yeats dreamed of going and living like Thoreau."

"Oh, I love Yates," Nanny says. "*Revolutionary Road* blew me away."

"William Butler," Alice says. "Not Richard."

"We would have been neighbors," Nanny says. "You would have loved my curried chicken salad."

"I make scrambled eggs."

"Bobbie dreamed big."

"It never would have worked," Alice says. "Doing things en masse rarely does."

"Yeah." Nanny nods. "But I can't see myself tooling up Madison Avenue on the arm of a health-care worker in a polyester pantsuit, can you?"

"The New York City Odd Couple," Alice says.

"And those old-people Marriotts where they have Sadie Hawkins Night? I'd rather move to Molokai."

"A hotel suite with a special monthly rate?" Alice suggests.

"So everyone could visit and order up room service?"

"Well, you needn't worry about aging," Alice says. "You've got a daughter."

"Right." Nanny nods. "And all those people in assisted living, they only have sons? Not that I'm seriously worried. We're the boomer generation, Alice. We're crap-intolerant. We changed the world. Civil rights, the EPA, gay power, they were under our watch. By the time we're old, we'll have a gazillion options."

"True," Alice agrees. "We're a force."

"We'll march. Why do you suppose our kids don't march? It bothers me."

"There's no draft."

"But we didn't march just to protect our own. We marched for everybody. Why are kids so passive now? What's going on?"

"What they worry about, they can't march for."

"What's that?"

"A health plan."

Nanny points her fork at the last bite of strawberry tart. "Want this?"

"It's yours."

"Was Bobbie involved with your boys?"

"They showed her their tests."

The Imaging Office has rows of gray seats. It reminds Nanny of an airport lounge. She settles down with *People* and tries not to make eye contact with anyone. She is glad to have the details of that day, glad Bobbie had Alice. She is glad to do this for Alice who did it for Bobbie. She believes no woman should go to these things alone. It is too much to bear alone. Nanny gets an idea. An escort service for women. Knowledgeable, compassionate women would accompany frightened women to appointments with the gynecologist, the divorce lawyer. Fate Dates for mammograms and barium swallows.

Fifteen minutes later, Alice flies into the waiting room. Her face is contorted. Her blouse misbuttoned.

"Safe for another year," she says, and bursts into tears.

25 · A Lovely Melon

"We could try for a second loan," Mr. Fleischman says.

This is the third time today he has suggested a second loan.

"You keep saying that, Mr. Fleischman."

"As I recall, your husband has a decent credit rating."

"I will not ask him again. That is not an option. He's been too good to Luba already."

"Well then, think about getting it yourself."

We've been going over the books since nine this morning. Surrounded by towers of Hefty reject bags, the two of us strategize in the wayback.

"I need collateral for a loan, Mr. Fleischman."

"Your apartment. Is it in your name too?"

"Surely you're not suggesting I gamble with my home."

"Your inventory. What's the current value?"

"My inventory is worth whatever I can get for it, Mr. Fleischman."

"What about moving?"

"Luba?"

"Someplace less expensive. Your rent is killing you, Alice. And it ain't going down."

"Mr. Fleischman. I believe you know. Luba has been at this location since 1937."

"You could rent a place on First Avenue and cut your nut in half."

"My clients don't shop First Avenue."

"Then what about upstairs, a second floor? Stay on Madison and move to the second floor."

"My clients don't do stairs."

Is that pity on his face? It is. Mr. Fleischman is pitying me.

"Well I'm getting a little low on ideas. What does Charlotte say? Have you discussed this with Charlotte?"

"This is my business now, Mr. Fleischman. Exclusively. My mother has severed all connections."

"Charlotte has a good *kopf.* How is my darling girl?"

I turn off the hot plate and pour Mr. Fleischman fresh tea. Praise God for Yumi. She has been alone out front all day. I offer Mr. Fleischman a *langue de chat.* Did he really chase Mother around this table? There is no room to chase anybody in the way-back. How old is Mr. Fleischman? Accountants age differently from other people. He could be eighty, he could be forty. Eventually all accountants look like Uriah Heep. Something happens to their backs.

Luba's lease is up. It must be renegotiated. The news isn't good. Mr. Fleischman wants me to close. What else am I good at? What else could I do? Rekindle "The Influence of the Occult Aesthetic of William Butler Yeats on Virginia Woolf's *The Waves*"? Surely someone has done the Yeats-Woolf occult-aesthetic *Waves* connection. And after all this time could I be a student again? Suppose I did complete my doctorate? Then what? A sixty-two-year-old TA?

"Why don't you ask your husband to spring for a second loan? Think about it, missy. He's a lawyer, am I right?"

"Mr. Fleischman," I say, "my husband does not work for a big law firm. My husband is in private practice."

"He doesn't have partners?"

"Not a one."

"He pays himself?"

"My husband is a solo practitioner."

"I'm so sorry," Mr. Fleischman says. "The world is full of greedy lawyers. We need more men like him."

Mr. Fleischman is trying to be helpful. Charles would sign for a second loan. All I'd have to do is ask. But do I want us to take that risk? Do I want to keep a mordant enterprise on life support? Is it possible New York doesn't need a gently preowned-designer boutique anymore? Where are New York's chic, clever women shopping now?

Mr. Fleischman shrugs on his coat. "I want you to consider a new lease with a sublet clause," he says. "You'd forfeit the business but the income from the sublet would pay off your debt. You might even be able to sell the business and make something though to tell you the truth, your books don't look so hot. Think about it." He reaches for his hat. "And when you see your mother, give her a big fat kiss from me."

He leaves. I call Mother.

"Do you need anything from the market?"

"Don't come, Alice."

"Of course I'm coming. How about a lovely melon? A cavaillon."

"Alice. I have Gristede's. I pick up the phone, the melon is here."

"All right, Mother. I'll see you at five, then."

"You never listen to me, Alice. I said *don't come.*"

"But it's Wednesday."

"It's four-thirty, and where is Tawny?"

"I don't care if your nails aren't done. Thursday is inventory. Friday I've got pickups and the notes."

"Talk to me for a few minutes, Alice. That will be enough. Wasn't Fleischman there today?"

"Yes."

"What did he have to say?"

"The usual."

"Tell me what Luba is wearing."

"Yumi is working on her right now. I had her in vintage Beene.

Mother, I had to laugh when it came in. It's a dress you had in 1968."

"The Empire ecru *crêpe de laine* with the navy *peau-de-soie* self-tie dickie?"

"The very one."

"What size, Alice?"

"Eight."

"Well it's not mine. I never wore something that huge in my life. Not even when I was carrying you."

"Mother, come see what Yumi and I are doing. It's exciting. Yumi is constructing clothes for Luba. You'd be very happy if you could see the store. And you could, you know, Mother."

"I will never expose myself in a wheelchair. Never. And I will never discuss this again. You will never bring it up again. I believe this was agreed upon last time. Now tell me. What do you hear from the boys?"

"David and Susan are coming east for Christmas. Camille and Jason are expecting any minute. Did I tell you the baby's head is down?"

"My child is going to be a grandmother. To think."

"Yes."

"Alice. I want you to remember this: When it is happening, it seems like it will never end. And when it ends, it seems like it was over in five minutes."

"What, Mother?"

"*Tout.*"

"*Maman,* is there nothing I can get you? Why don't I send over some black-and-white cookies? You adore those."

"I'm tired, Alice. You can't get me anything. Tell me a story. I'd like to drift off."

"All right, Mother. A story. Let's see. All right. Once upon a time, Mother, there was a very beautiful woman. She was a size four and sometimes in couture, a two, and she had perfect taste.

People came from all over the world to see what she was wearing. She could spin clothes out of spiderwebs and moss. Her hair was the color of hay and curled like a lamb's. One day a handsome stranger rode into town on a white horse. He saw the girl and fell in love with her on the spot. He asked at the local café, 'Who's the girl with hair the color of hay curled like a lamb's?' 'She's the spinner,' he was told. 'Every day she goes into the woods and spins.' The next morning, the handsome man waited for her to walk into the woods and then he followed her. He watched her gather webs and those fluffy white dandelion heads and soft green pads of moss and bits of thyme. She threw them all up in the air, and when they came down, they were a cloth luminous as the moon on a river. The man had to decide then and there if he was going to exploit her and corner the market in this glowing cloth or whether he was going to live a quiet life with her and her secret power and give up the chance to be a fabric czar. Mother . . . Mother?"

I rinse out Fleischman's cup. Winding through reject bags toward the front, I hear shouting. It's coming from the store. A woman screams. I never should have left Yumi alone.

I grab Jason's bat and charge through the curtains. Luba is packed. Women are pulling sweaters over their heads, not waiting for a dressing room. Women in thongs, women in nothing, shimmy into dresses and shriek, "That's mine!,", "I saw it first!" Young women who have never patronized Luba are trying on combos. They're pushing their way to the mirrors and admiring each other. I look outside. There is a line.

Yumi dashes back and forth, arms loaded with clothes. She studies a customer, sails something at her, then runs to the racks for more. They blow her kisses. She blows back. It's a feeding frenzy. In the window, Luba stands majestic in a . . . what? The collar is a deep Peter Pan cut from a fisherman's sweater. The skirt is half plaid kilt, half lamé. Lace sleeves poke through a weskit made of a woven silver handbag. Beneath the weskit is a—a—a bra? A bandeau? Glorified pasties? Two stuffed blue leather gloves joined by a chain cup Luba's breasts. It looks as if hands are grabbing her. Yumi has put a canteloupe where Luba's head would be if Luba had one.

26 · The Arbiter of Everything

I hate the fake flowers. No matter what season it is, there they are, desiccating in my lobby. I hate the fake verdigris on the fake-bronze urn that holds the fake flowers too. Most of all, I hate one fake flower: the dusty brown seedpod that looks like extraterrestrial Swiss cheese. Does someone on our co-op board think extraterrestrial Swiss cheese increases the value of our shares?

"How are you, Mrs. Wunderlich," Joe says, holding the door. He tips his hat. "Have a nice evening."

Joe assumes I'm in for the night. Doormen know everything.

I skim the mail and hang up my coat. From the foyer, I see straight through the living room. No carpets, no drapes, lots of light. A broken-in sofa, the coffee table that used to have an oak pedestal Freddy sawed down in the kitchen. Granny Esther's ebony upright Flora took lessons on. The oil portrait above it of my eternally young mother. Chairs that don't match, some wear shawls. What this room has is family history. Not that you need a family for family history. With enough money, a decorator can give an orphan a past.

In the kitchen I put up decaf. A brown paper filter neats into the cone. Bobbie used Bounty: "You can do a lot more with paper towel than you think." She brewed her own glass cleaner with vinegar. How to explain another person's ferrety economies? Bobbie was the only woman I know who never worried about money, who worked purely for pleasure. She called Jack "a cash bull." And here I am. When Social Security kicks in, it won't cover my HBO, my CNN, my *HMO*.

The mail. Predictable bills. My college wants to be remembered in my will. The Sierra Club would like something too. The Sanctuary of Abraham and Sarah is encouraging me to "PLAN AHEAD AND SAVE!" on a plot. Two sex-toy catalogs—thanks, Bobbie. And two of those old-age ones. Did Social Security tip them off? Soft World and Golden Gals, catalogs with products to escort me gently into that sweet night. Moisturizing booties, rubber sheets. What I need is a catalog for widows. "*Solo*," I'll call it. What do you say, Freddy? Good idea? Right. You'd start singing: "Dream, Dream, Dream."

"Solo, the Catalog for Women Without Men."

"Flying Solo, for Women Who Wing It."

What would I put in it? A back zipper-puller and WD-40. What else does a manless woman need?

Williams-Sonoma. L. L. Bean. What's this? How odd. An envelope with my handwriting. I run my thumb under the flap:

Dear Ms. Wunderlich,
    Alas, I have no knowledge of your friend Roberta Bloom. I certainly do wish you every good luck in your search.
    All best, Haney Jeff Watts

Black Blobs isn't him. One down, unless he's breathing a sigh of relief: *I'm safe now. My wife will never know.*

What did she want? I know what the Glogowers want. Poor kids. The only things moving are nine million and up. Trophy apartments owned by leveraged-buyout kings with vacant castles all over the world, everything swaddled in white sheets, furniture mausoleums.

Death, taxes, and the widening gap. Twenty-nine years I've been here. This apartment is worth more than I could ever afford now but I don't have enough to refinish the floors. That's the new definition of rich, Freddy: someone who could afford their apartment *now*. We couldn't. Neither could half our neighbors. The new Wall Streeters in the building, with their limos downstairs? What I'll earn the rest of my life wouldn't make their down payments.

But if I sold this place, where would I go? Flora took her first steps here. The only way I'll leave is in a body bag. Could I live somewhere else? Of course I *could*. I just don't want to feel forced out by economics. Though maybe I might be ready to sort of consider it, ready*ish*. I could entertain the thought.

One thing for sure: I have too much room. If the world were fair, a young family would be living here. There would be noise in the apartment again. Laughing. Running. Dried apple-juice rinks on the floor. How strange it is when your apartment goes quiet. It's as if they have lives.

I stare out the window. The man across the way is eating either a bowl of cereal or soup. He pours milk in it. It's cereal. He's watching *CSI*. A boy has opened a mailbox and a human head is in it. What could be sadder than eating cereal alone in front of a forensic-medical show? *Watching* someone eat cereal alone in front of a forensic-medical show.

During the commercial, the man gets up. He strolls into his bathroom and kicks off his shorts. He flosses his teeth in the mirror. He pulls his lips back, stretching his neck to check if his gums are bleeding.

Then he looks out his window.

Our eyes meet.

He waves and wiggles his hips.

The naked man can see me?

I am sick of the naked man. I need something new to look at. Bobbie would say, "So haul your butt out of there already." The

Arbiter of Everything would push. "You'll never have to think about money again."

I find my Rolodex. I lift my thumb under the G tab. "Hello, Meredith?" I say. "It's Nanny Wunderlich. I know you're on bed rest, but any chance you and Steve could see one more place?"

One day you're so sure of something. And the next day you're profoundly sure of the opposite.

27 · Age Is a Benefit

I ring the bell again. Where is Murlene? Bathing Mother? "Hello?"
I let myself in. "Hello! Mother?" She is not in bed. I knock on her
bathroom door. No answer. I open it slowly, fearing the worst.

"*Maman?* Murlene?"

They are nowhere. I check the closet in the foyer. The wheelchair is gone. I am about to call downstairs and see if Mother was
rushed off in an ambulette when I notice a piece of her notepaper
on the console.

"Darling," it reads. "You did not answer your cell phone. Mr.
Fleischman came by and insisted I accompany him to the Comme
des Garcons show at FIT. I wish you could have seen me—the
Dior black paramatta with the Hattie Carnegie cloche, Chanel
patent cap-toes, the Schreiner japanned brooch, and the Dali-
Schiaparelli illuminated handbag. *Formidable!* Love, Mother."

> *And pluck till times and times are done*
> *The silver apples of the moon,*
> *The golden apples of the sun*

"Sorry to have missed you," I jot beneath. "Love, Alice."

I press the cell phone on. Going down in the elevator I think, I
must call Roberta. We'll have such a good laugh. Then I remember. There is no one to tell. No one else could begin to understand.

Oh Roberta darling. Had I not grown up with you, would we
have been friends? The first time you whispered, "Don't tell so-

166

and-so I told you," I would have written you off. From the time we were little girls, you told secrets. When I confided I loved Henry Mishkin, you told Henry Mishkin, my seminal shock. The women I like now do not carry tales. Age is a benefit. You know in a moment if a woman is friend material. You were, what?, grand-mothered in. I am sixty-two. Life is in shorthand. Were I to meet you today, Roberta, who knows if we would be friends.

When I get home, the phone is ringing. VOGEL, J, the ID says.

"Jason?"

"We're in labor, Mom."

"Where are you, darling?"

"Admissions. They're taking us to the labor room."

We. Us. "Are you staying with Camille, Jason? How is she?"

"Of course I'm staying with her. Don't worry, Mom. I'm not eating the placenta. Wait. Hold a sec. Camille wants to say something."

Oh no. What is appropriate? Good luck? Break a leg?

"Alice?"

"Hello, dear. How are you feeling?"

"I feel wonderful," she says. "Excited. Exhilarated. I'm seven centimeters dilated and the contractions are three minutes apart and the doctor says I'm effaced and my mucous plug came out at ten-forty-seven this morning."

What on earth is a mucous plug? "Well I couldn't be happier, dear."

"Sure you could," Camille says. "When you hold your new grandchild. Alice?"

"Yes?"

"Thank you for making Jason. Thank you for making this possible."

"Oh." I close my eyes. I feel weak. "The two of you . . . Both of you . . . A baby . . . Oh my . . . my *dears.*"

"Alice, why don't you get your tickets?"

"When do you want us to come?"

I hear her panting a coast away. In the distance Jason shouts, "Want ice?" Then "Want the back pillow?" Camille yells "Nooooooooooo!" Jason says, "A lollipop?" Camille screams, "Fuck the lollipop!"

"Mom," Jason says into the phone, "can you come the day after tomorrow? That's when we'll really need help. We've got a doula but we need you."

"Shall we bring your perambulator? It's down in the bin."

"What's a perambulator? Gotta go. We're starting to Breathe."

I must always remember this moment. I must pin this moment like a butterfly. This moment is all I ever wanted. All I ever wanted was transcendence.

I call Charles. "Charles? . . . I . . . We . . ."

"What's the matter?" he says, alarmed.

"Camille is in labor. Oh, Charles. They want us to come."

"When?"

"Thursday."

"I'll take care of everything." I knew Charles would say that. "Loveya."

I roll our suitcases out of the hall closet. When they're fairly well packed, I leave a note for the cleaning lady. I turn on the shower and test the water. Wonderful. I step in and soap a washcloth. A baby. I am going to be a grandmother. A new generation. Jason is going to be a father. My baby is having a baby. I will hold the future in my arms again.

Water pummels my back. I lower my head so it beats my nape. Remember this moment, Alice. Remember it when the call comes about Mother. I turn and bend my head back so water drills my forehead. Remember this when the doctor says, "I think we need more tests." I open my mouth. Remember it when Charles no

longer recognizes you and your knees won't let you run the Drive.
Remember this moment. That you had it.

I want to laugh it feels so good. I stand there, water pounding
down. My son a father. I pour shampoo in my palm. A baby, a
whole new life. In two days I'll be rubbing shampoo on a baby's
head again and, unless the baby's bald, making devil's horns.

I suds my hair. There is a flap of cold, a shift in the air. My
breasts are being cupped from behind. Charles has joined me in
the shower. He presses up against me and hooks his chin over my
shoulder.

"Alice," he says.

His breath smells like Colgate.

28 · The Way Perfume Is Applied

Nanny pauses in the doorway of a restaurant. A man has arranged to meet her at the bar. She has enjoyed the process of getting ready. It has been three years since she has gotten ready for a man, experienced that specific kind of excitement, the modifications in a woman's routine when she is anticipating the gaze of a man. The way perfume is applied.

She arrives at the restaurant five minutes late. She has predetermined that if he is not there she will wait five more minutes. Not at the bar as planned, but at the reservation podium where the maître d' stands. She has never sat at a bar alone. She never wants to. There are things you can do to make yourself feel lonelier and she is meticulous about avoiding them.

"May I help you?" the maître d' says.

"I'm supposed to be meeting a Mr. Abrams."

The maître d' turns toward the bar. A man looks up. He smiles and rises off the stool.

"Nanny?"

She extends her hand. "Ben?"

"Let me take your coat," he says.

She turns. He slips it off her shoulders and hands it to the maître d'.

"Were you waiting long?" she asks.

"No," he says.

Her husband, she thinks, would have said, "That depends. How do you define 'long'?"

"My daughter is going to be overjoyed when I tell her we've met." Nanny roosts on a stool.

"Flora and Dahlia are great plotters," Ben says. "What can I get you to drink?"

Nanny has not ordered a drink in a long time. She does not like plain hard liquor. Wine will make her face turn red.

She searches her brain for what she used to drink in college. A drink from the past before she drank wine. But nothing that will get her drunk and make her say stupid things. Not a Twister. No. A Strangler? A *Stinger.* Definitely not a Stinger.

Ben watches her think. After careful consideration, Nanny says, "I'd like an apricot-brandy Collins with grenadine."

"Two apricot-brandy Collinses with grenadine," Ben says.

The bartender squares paper napkins in front of them.

Nanny smiles at Ben. She can't think of one thing to say. Her daughter was right. He has hair. It is cut short on the sides and it is gray. Her daughter did not mention the mustache. That is gray too. She has never kissed a man with a mustache. It makes her think of William Powell. He has blue eyes, and though he is not wrinkled in a crosshatched way, vertical lines form parentheses around his mouth, deep grooves men get women don't.

Ben studies Nanny. He's relieved she is not one of those women with fake red nails. He was concerned about that. He has taken out claw women and even though he is suspicious of generalizations, their conversation often drifts toward money. They have gewgaws in their handbags they primp with while you're talking to them. He is grateful too that Nanny has flesh on her bones. He had to close his eyes when he made love to Hannah. Her thighs were sticks. Ben has come to believe that skinny women with fake red nails who carry objects with logos in their pocketbooks are the kiss of death.

The drinks come. Nanny recalls they used to have umbrellas. She is pleased the Maraschino cherry is still there.

"Want mine?" Ben plucks his stem.

"Sure."

They talk about their daughters. They talk about their daughters' terrible apartments. They talk about how hard it is for young people in New York today and whether it's good or bad to under-write them a little bit.

"I think of Dahlia at *Visage,* that her job there is kind of an extension of her education and I'm happy to subsidize that."

"What our girls are learning at the magazine will enable them to eventually get a job that pays a decent wage."

"Amen," Ben says.

"Gone are the days when your rent was a quarter of your salary," Nanny says.

They tell how they met their spouses, but they do not venture into their marriages. The conversation flows the way it does between two strangers who have no reason not to like each other. Nanny finds it pleasant sipping drinks at a bar with a person gen-uinely interested in what she has to say, a person who can build on an idea. Ben has seen the *Who Copied Whom?* show. He has a generous spirit about it. He says things are in the air, that often artists work the same turf without knowing what other artists are doing. He cites two comparisons, sparing Nanny the need to find examples. "Remember *Deliverance,*" he says. "And *That Champi-onship Season?* What about Damien Hirst and Martin McDonagh?"

Nanny agrees.

"What do you think?" he asks. "Will 9/11 influence everything across the boards? Will Katrina?"

"I don't know," Nanny says. "Societal evolution is different from cataclysmic events. For instance, did any great art come out of the Holocaust? I don't think so. It's just too big, too ungraspable. Too terrible."

"What about Primo Levi?" he says. "*Bent.* Paul Celan? Elie Wiesel? What about Philip Guston and Conrad Richter? Louis Begley? Sebald? Kiefer? Cynthia Ozick? What about *The Diary of Anne Frank?*"

"Anne Frank's diary isn't art," Nanny says. "It's a personal account that's become an icon."

"Does it have to be conceived as art to be art?"

"Yes," Nanny says. "I think so."

"What about African masks? What about Duchamp? What about the Venus of Willendorf?"

"Things that weren't created to be art? Things that had a purpose we now think of as art?"

"Yeah."

And so it went.

Nanny finds him easy to talk to. He looks her in the eye when he speaks. He's animated. But when she tries to picture herself in bed with him, even kissing him, she can't.

Ben appreciates her no-nonsense quality. Not that she is blunt or crude. No. She strikes him as a woman who would not blithely lie and better yet, not willingly hurt somebody. She is easy in her skin. He likes her perfume. It smells like flowers but she didn't drown herself in it. He catches a whiff whenever she moves. He imagines she is the kind of woman who can laugh in bed. When she laughs, she leans forward and her left eyebrow goes up. Ben finds himself trying to make it go up.

"Would you like another drink?" he asks.

"No thank you."

He checks his watch. Nanny thinks he's been very polite to spend so much time with her. He has manners. She has no idea if he enjoyed her company and it doesn't really matter. She has gotten her first date since Freddy's death over with. It was not a disaster. It was pleasant. She liked dressing for a man again and being with a man, seeing his eyes widen when he spotted you. It was wonderful making a man laugh again, him wanting to make you laugh.

He looks up from his watch and signals the bartender. Nanny anticipates him saying, "It was nice to meet you."

"I'm starving," he says. "Have you had dinner yet?"

.   .   .

Nanny's apartment is dark. She flips the light switch and goes through the mail. It's a week before Christmas, and Harry and David are pushing grapefruit. A takeout menu. More bills. Two envelopes in her own handwriting.

She opens the first one. Written below her signature on the letter she mailed him, George Bemis has scribbled:

Sorry! The name doesn't ring a bell. Is this a former student?
GB

She opens the other envelope.

Dear Ms. Wunderlich,
 I knew Roberta Heumann Bloom quite well. You can reach me at drawl@duke.edu
 Sincerely, Dale Rawlinson

29 · What She Wanted

The maître d' smiles. His favorite ladies are back. It has been months since he has seen either of them with the other woman. He fears the worst. The last time he saw that woman, she was wearing a turban.

He likes these two. They know his name. They order the same thing each time, and the one with the bangs leaves a six-dollar tip on a fifteen dollar salad.

He nods to a small table.

"Actually, Michael, we're expecting a gentleman," Alice says.

"Well good for you!" He leads them to a four.

They sit side by side, their backs against the banquette. They want to see Dale when he comes in.

The waitress removes the fourth place setting. "Can I get you some Perrier?"

Alice turns to Nanny. "Shall we celebrate?"

"Are we picking up the tab?"

Alice smiles. "Do you suppose our late friend's lover expects to be treated?"

"For Bobbie's sake, I hope not."

Alice unfolds her napkin. "Did you bring the letter?"

Nanny pats her purse. "What if he doesn't show?"

"Bergdorf's has extraordinary sale racks."

"I'm in."

"Something occurred to me," Alice says. "Did you notice any-one unusual at the funeral? A Southern gentleman?"

"What would that be?" Nanny asks. "Colonel Sanders? No. I was bawling. It was SRO. Remember?"

"Packed to the gills. Roberta kept up with everybody. Teachers. Patients. School friends. Frankly, Nanny? It amazed me she made time for me."

"There were tons of people in her life."

"But the two of us, we're the ones she trusted."

"She left Dale to us."

"What a precise way to put that."

Nanny checks her watch. "He's three minutes late."

A young woman sails in, rosy, full of life. Eyes follow her.

"We have something she'd kill to have," Alice remarks.

"We do?"

"Perspective."

"Ah."

"I had a thought, Nanny."

"What?"

"That Roberta told other people's secrets to protect her own."

"How you figure?"

"A smoke screen. A way to avoid discussing her private life. You can't talk about yourself if you're talking about someone else."

"You think Bobbie had lots of secrets?" Nanny asks.

"It's a possibility."

"All the stuff she blabbed, the Jack stories, that was a cover?"

" 'Stories,' " Alice says, "is the operative word."

"So how was your trip?" Nanny asks. "How's the baby?"

Alice closes her eyes. "A whole new life."

"Morgan is—what—six weeks?"

Alice nods.

"Any pictures?"

"They don't do that anymore, Nanny. Photos come in e-mails now."

"Grandmas have to lug around computers?"

The model spins in front of them. She looks like an ice-cream cone. Waffled brown fabric tapers so tightly around her calves, she walks as if her feet are bound.

They watch her hobble to another table.

Laughing, they don't notice the person standing at theirs.

"Nanny and Alice, I presume?"

"I'm Nanny," Nanny says.

"Yes?" Alice says.

"Dale Rawlinson."

A woman with dark eyebrows extends a hand. "It's a great pleasure to meet you both."

"Excuse me," Nanny says. "You're Dale?"

"Last time I looked."

They shake.

"I'm Alice Vogel," Alice says.

"Kind of figured that."

"You're Dale Rawlinson?" Nanny says.

"That's my name."

"Please, Dale," Alice says, "come sit down."

Dale pulls out a chair. It screeches against the stone floor.

"We're thrilled you could make it," Alice says.

Nanny's mind races. "How did you know it was us?"

"Bertie gave me your pictures." Dale takes in the scene. "So this is Bergdorf Goodman's. She was fond of this place."

"It's where we met for lunch," Alice says.

"And where we continue to keep the flame, Professor Rawlinson," Nanny adds.

"Please call me Dale." She pronounces it "Day-el." She leans in, looks from Nanny to Alice and says, "Well?"

Nanny can't think of anything to say. Neither can Alice.

Dale waits.

"You said you had to be in New York?" Nanny ventures.

"An auction of Civil War prosthetics. I've got my eye on an articulated hand. Belonged to a man shot in the wrist August 16, 1864. The Battle of Deep Bottom in Virginia."

The waitress hovers.

"I wouldn't mind giving that salad Bertie loved a whirl."

"We'd like three Gothams," Alice orders.

"Listen." Dale holds up a finger. "Bach. Bertie loved the three B's. Bach. Beethoven. And Billie."

Nanny smiles.

Dale straightens the salt and pepper shakers. "You know," she says, "Bertie loved you girls to kingdom come. She loved you girls, she loved Betsy, she loved that husband of hers too. She loved Flora and she loved your boys, Alice. She loved her work. She loved her life and she made room to love me too. I suppose she had enough love to light the world. And in fact," Dale says, "for me she did."

"Why didn't she tell us about you?" Nanny asks.

"She thought about it. She thought about it. You all did so much together with Jack and Betsy. In the end she believed it would be a burden."

"There's something I need to know, Dale," Alice says. "Were you aware of her condition?"

"Yes, I knew. Course I knew."

"We were concerned about that," Alice says. "We weren't certain about the time frame."

"I saw Bertie in the hospital right before she went home. The last time she went home."

"How?" Nanny asks. "I was there every day."

"She worked it all out. Real artful, our girl. For Bertie it was fun breaking the rules. Told me to get my hands on some blue scrubs and waltz in after visiting hours. We spent the whole night together. That was the last time I saw her. Don't cry, darlin'." Dale squeezes Nanny's hand. "Bertie didn't cry. Not in front of me. Not one tear. I never met a human being on the face of God's earth who could wring so much from a moment."

"She never complained," Nanny says.

"Nope."

"Once I asked her if it was hell," Alice says.

"What did she say?" Dale asks.

" 'Dante's or Milton's?' "

"I just loved her. Always will."

"Even though she loved her husband?" Nanny asks.

"Why Nanny," Dale smiles, "surely you don't surmise the complexities and capabilities of the heart preclude any style of loving."

Nanny searches for a response. "I'm happy Bobbie had every drop of love she had."

Alice tries to envision Roberta's head next to Dale's on a pillow. "How did you meet?" she asks.

"In a Dollar Store."

Bent over the table, the women talk. Lunchers casually observing them would think they were old friends. Someone looking a bit closer might suspect the three women somehow didn't go together the way old friends meeting for lunch do. They dress too differently and their levels of intensity are widely various. But another person? A suggestible person with a proclivity for wondering? That person would discern that two of the women did not know the third. They would know this because two of the women sit a bit stiffly whereas the third is enjoying herself without reservation. And someone else eyeing the trio? A person with burnished experience? That person might note: These disparate women have a marked similarity. They radiate the same intellect.

Dale continues the story of how they met: "She was in Durham for a meeting. That's where I work. I teach American History at Duke."

"She loved the Dollar Store," Nanny says. "I bet she was getting eyeglasses, right? She hated her contacts."

"Well, don't I know!" Dale says. "Made me plain crazy. What if a doctor tried to pry her contacts out and she wasn't wearing them? I told Bertie those bracelets needed editing. You girls got them on?"

Alice and Nanny hold out their wrists. Dale cradles the edge of their palms and runs her thumbs over the words.

"You were in the Dollar Store . . ." Alice picks up the thread.

"There she was, standing at the readers display, spinning it round and round, trying on one pair after another. This one, that one." Dale shakes her head. "She looked so fine, checking the mirror, trying another pair. Tossing them in the cart like there was going to be a war and you wouldn't be able to get readers."

"She used to say, 'Why buy one pair for thirty when you can get thirty pairs for one?' " Nanny explains.

Dale continues: "So she kept trying on glasses and I told her which ones looked good. Fact is, they all looked good."

Nanny asks, "How many did she get?"

Dale thinks. "I believe it was a baker's dozen."

"Each room had its own pair."

"Each handbag," Alice adds.

"Each pocket."

"I adored her," Dale says.

"So did we," Alice says.

"She understood better than I did the nature of what we had."

"How do you mean?" Nanny asks.

"That it couldn't be sustained. She always said that what happened between us was in a bubble. That if the real world intruded, the bubble had to burst."

"Did you agree?" Nanny asks.

"Not at first."

"Then?"

"She was right. What we had, it's always inflated by the difficulty, raw need that, for one reason or another, can't be met. And once it's easy? Once it's everyday? Well the best it can be is most likely what you already have. Once circumstances no longer heighten the situation, all you're left with is plain ho-hum don't-forget-to-pick-up-the-laundry life. Bertie knew. Think of the great love stories. Now you girls tell me. What would have happened if Romeo set up house with Juliet?"

"Bored to tears in six months," Alice says.

" 'What? The Capulets are coming to dinner *again*?' " Nanny adds.

Their Gothams arrive. Dale looks puzzled. "What is this?"

"Chopped salad," Alice says.

"Well where's the greens?"

"They're in there," Nanny says. "Trust me. This is Bergdorf's. They do everything but chew it for you."

Dale takes a taste. The women watch. She puts down her fork. "I get it," she says.

"Are you aware Roberta left us a letter?"

Dale nods.

"Do you have any letters from Bobbie?" Nanny says.

"I shredded them. She didn't want any possibility of Jack and Betsy finding out."

"No one would have known if she'd burned your letter," Alice says. "So why didn't she?"

"Right," Nanny says. "What if we'd given Jack and Betsy your letter?"

"Bertie knew you wouldn't."

"She engineered this whole thing, didn't she?" Alice says. "She engineered it and saw the three of us having lunch here."

"Why Alice," Dale says. "Bertie said you'd say that."

They eat their salads. Dale asks how Betsy is doing. She inquires after Jack. She knows Nanny has lost her husband and asks if Alice's grandchild has been born yet and if there is any chance David and Jason might move back to New York. She asks if Flora is still the beauty director at *Visage*.

"Was Roberta at all concerned that Jack would find out?" Alice asks.

"Not a bit. Know what Bertie said? 'People only find out what you want them to find out.' "

"Think that's true?" Nanny says.

"You bet I do," Dale says. "Me, Bertie, and Herr Professor Freud."

The waitress stops by their table. "Still working on those?"

Dale puts her fork down. "Actually," she says, "I'm working on a book about a peg-leg whittler from Chattanooga." She turns to Nanny.

"And I'm working on a real-estate transaction."

"And I'm co-designing a line of clothes. But," Alice says, "we've finished our salads if you'd care to take our plates."

Nanny fishes in her bag for the letter.

"Why thank you." Dale opens her briefcase and puts it in. "And I have a little something for you, too."

She reaches into a pocket of her Norfolk jacket and extracts a square blue envelope. On the front is written: "To My Dearest Friends."

Nanny opens it and reads aloud:

Dearests. Congratulations! If you're reading this, you've found Dale. I had every faith the two of you working together would. That's my legacy to you. Have you figured that out yet? You are my darlings. What happens next is up to you. Now. Please take care of Jack and Betsy. Please take care of each other. Please rip this to bits. That's the last thing you have to do for me.

Love you to pieces,
Your Friend to the End and, Apparently, Beyond.

30 · The Rest

She mounts the carton like it's a horse. She straddles it. She takes a deep breath, flattens her palms on top of the towels, and presses down. She pushes in with her thighs until the corrugated flaps touch. She yanks a swath of silver duct tape. It makes a ripping sound. She stretches her arm to hold it taut enough to cut. Something happens. The strip flies up and grips the sleeve of her sweater. When she tries to rip it off, the duct tape catches her bangs. Nanny's arm is duct taped to her forehead.

"Help!" she shouts.

Alice wanders out of the living room where she has been packing LPs. "Good Lord!"

They wrestle Nanny's sleeve. Strand by strand, Alice pulls Nanny's hair off the adhesive.

Nanny does not want to waste the piece. She tries to close the box with it, but that section of the duct tape is covered with fuzz balls. Duct tape as sweater de-piller, she thinks. Duct tape as depilatory?

LINENS, she Magic Markers five sides of the box. She tries to imagine her new bed in the new apartment, a bed only she will have slept on. She tries to imagine herself making the new bed with new sheets, and what it will be like not seeing the pear tree that has measured time and the seasons for more than half her life. She imagines not seeing the naked man in the shower cap again. Now she will see plane trees with bark mottled like camouflage. A much smaller apartment with a much better view.

The new apartment is four blocks north. Even so, the ZIP code is different. The neighborhood is in transition. SpaHa for Spanish Harlem? TheBa for The Barrio? UpYors for Upper Yorkville? Four blocks in New York, another world.

Flora walks into the bedroom carrying a Teflon-coated pan in one hand and an aluminum drip coffee pot with a glass knob in the other. "Mom?"

"That's a coffeepot, darling," Nanny says. "Specifically, that was your grandmother's coffeepot. Granny Esther used that every morning before there was electric."

"How did it work?"

Nanny dismounts. She pulls the lid up by its hollow glass knob. She lifts the round coffee basket off the spindle. "You put water in the pot. You put the coffee in this basket. You put the cover back on the basket and the lid back on the pot. You set it on the stove. When the water boiled, you turned down the flame and the water pushed up this tube and spilled over into the grounds, and it kept pushing up again and again until it was coffee. You could tell by the smell. But you had to watch it."

"Say you're joking, Ma."

"They called it googling, I mean burbling, I mean *percolating*. Don't toss that, sweetie."

"But you've got an electric drip, Mom. I can sell this for you on eBay."

"I know. But I like to look at it."

Flora waves her other hand. "Okay. What about this?"

"Daddy and I got that skillet free when we got married. The banks gave out gifts in those days when you opened a savings account. That skillet has sautéed thirty-two years of memories."

"Mom. You have to know what's important and what's sentimental."

"Sentimental is important."

"You can't keep this, Mom. I won't let you. The Teflon is all scratched. This pan is poison."

"Okay, okay." Nanny gives up. "Out."

The women work with the windows open. It's April. The air smells green. Birds chirp like they're at a party. Now and then, a white petal wafts in, loses momentum, settles on the floor. It's the kind of New York morning people leave home an hour early so they can walk where they are going.

After the last box is sealed and labeled, Flora kisses her mother goodbye.

"But Alice and I want to take you to lunch," Nanny says.

"I'm meeting Teddy." Flora beams.

"Oh, sweetheart! Take a good look then. This is where you grew up. This was your first home."

"I did look, Mom."

"Want me to walk through it with you one last time?"

"I know where I cut my chin on the radiator cover, Ma. I know where you found the Brussels sprouts I hid."

"Well if you ever want to see it again, sweetheart, the Glogow-ers said you've got an open invitation."

Nanny looks for Alice. She's in the kitchen scrubbing the stovetop.

"You don't have to do that," Nanny says. " 'Broom clean.' That means 'swept.' "

Alice peels off one yellow rubber glove, then the other. She places them side by side on the rim of the sink.

"Sure you don't mind me staying over?" Nanny asks. "It's just till the paint dries."

"Charles and I are looking forward to it," Alice says.

Nanny takes in her kitchen. Her eyes stop on the depression

in the molding Flora's high chair rubbed that no painter could plump. She remembers the excitement the day the fridge with the ice-cube dispenser in the door arrived. She sees herself bent over the oven, pulling out meatloaf after meatloaf, year after year. She remembers the night she got so angry at her husband words failed and she threw chocolate pudding at him. They stripped to clean the mess and wound up making chocolate-covered love.

This is the last time Nanny will be in this kitchen. Her life has no defined arc. This she welcomes. What used to terrify her excites her. She is uncertain what her dreams are. They could be anything. The day. A finite thing you get to live over and over. Every twenty-four hours you start fresh. You try to get it right. Every morning a chance to begin again.

"Funny," Alice says.

"What?"

"Everything."

"Think we knew the same person, Alice?"

"No. We knew her differently. Each of us knew an entirely different person."

"Think that's unusual?"

"Not anymore."

"We both thought we were her best friend, Alice."

"You and I and a hundred other people."

"I don't believe in jealousy," Nanny says.

"It's not my religion either," Alice agrees. "Strange."

"What?"

"The words for secrets. 'Dope.' 'Skinny.' "

" 'Poop.' 'Low-down,' " Nanny adds.

" 'Dirt.' 'Scuttlebutt.' All pejorative. When secrets are eminently worthwhile."

"How well did we know her, Alice?"

Alice considers before answering. "We knew what she wanted us to know. And I would not care to know more than that about anybody. Would you?"

"Do you think," Nanny asks, "we were as important to her as she was to us?"

"Does it matter?"

When the last box is sealed, Nanny bends over and pushes it to the front door. She presses her hands into her kidneys and stretches her back.

"Here we are," she says.

"Here we are," Alice agrees.

"What now?" Nanny asks.

Alice thinks. She says: "Lunch at Bergdorf's? A film at the Paris? The Steichen show at the Met? A walk around the reservoir followed by café au lait at EAT? Yoga at the Y? Tulips at the Conservatory Garden? The Aesthetic Movement show at the Cooper-Hewitt? Shopping for Morgan? Have you been to the Dahesh yet? Tea at Kai? A stroll down Madison? And then I thought we'd have dinner with Charles. And later?" Alice lays a soft hand on Nanny's wrist.

"Yes, later."

"After that?"

"After that."

"The rest?"

"The rest."

"The rest is up for grabs."

Acknowledgments

Thank you, Dr. Michael H. Cohen and Helen Vendler for sharing Yeats scholarship. Thank you, Peter Morgen Blitzer, Polly Volk Blitzer, Robby M. Browne, Pat Heller, Amy Hempel, Anita Lazar Plotkin, Chris Richter, Dr. Jay Rohrlich, Allen Staley, John Tauranac, Anne Truitt, and the Corporation of Yaddo. Thank you, Jo Ann Volk Lederman, M.S.Ed.LMFT, who has never lost a couple who wanted to stay together. Bless you, J. R. Humphreys, Raymond Kennedy, Sidney Offit, and Richard Yates. *Mille grazie,* Gloria Loomis. And Robin Desser, thank you from the center of my heart.

A Note About the Author

Patricia Volk is also the author of the memoir *Stuffed: Adventures of a Restaurant Family*, a James Beard Award nominee; the novel *White Light;* and two collections of short stories, *All It Takes* and *The Yellow Banana*. Her stories, book reviews, and essays have appeared in numerous publications, including the *New York Times, The Atlantic Monthly, New York, The New Yorker, Playboy, Redbook, GQ, The Quarterly,* and *O, The Oprah Magazine*. She was a weekly columnist for New York *Newsday*. Ms. Volk lives in New York City.

A Note on the Type

This book was set in Caledonia, a typeface designed by W. A. Dwiggins (1880–1956). It belongs to the family of printing types called "modern face" by printers—a term used to mark the change in style of the type letters that occurred around 1800. Caledonia borders on the general design of Scotch Roman but it is more freely drawn than that letter. This version of Caledonia was adapted by David Berlow in 1979.

Composed by
Creative Graphics,
Allentown, Pennsylvania

Printed and bound by
R. R. Donnelley & Sons,
Harrisonburg, Virginia

Designed by
Iris Weinstein